CUTOUT

MAX ALLAN COLLINS
BARBARA COLLINS

Illustrations and cover by
SONNY & BIDDY

Published by NeoText, 2024
Copyright © 2024 Max Allan Collins and Barbara Collins

All rights reserved. No part of this publication may be reproduced or transmitted in any form or by any means without permission of the publisher.

Foster children, in particular those who are never adopted, have common frailties — feelings of abandonment, low self-esteem, and a wariness to trust others; but they also can possess a fierce determination of self-preservation. I call this the Marilyn Monroe Syndrome.

— Helga W. Friedrich, PhD, MSW

The young woman had been at a party in SoHo and was just leaving the vegan restaurant when the torrential downpour came. Midnight, and no umbrella, no raincoat! Empty cabs would be hard to come by; Uber would be worse. Her new dress would be soaked, maybe ruined. Never mind – she could afford a new one. In the morning, she had to leave early for DC, and all she wanted now was to get back to her apartment.

At least the Spring Street Station wasn't far. She made a dash for the subway, disappearing into a black hole at the side of the brick Michael Kors Building, beneath the words

GOD'S LOVE WE DELIVER.

After descending the cement steps to the concrete floor (stained with whatever God had delivered there), she used her MetroCard at the turnstile, then hurried along the beige-tiled walls to the platform, where a train was waiting, but not patiently. Its doors closed before she could reach them, and then she was standing there, dripping, watching with a sigh as the tail-end of the train receded into the dark tunnel. She'd have to get the next one going uptown. She positioned herself beside an iron girder.

Only one other person was on the platform — gender nullified by an NYU hoodie – who she assumed was waiting for the next local train, and not an express to uptown. If she hadn't been annoyed by her circumstances, she might have been uneasy. Subways were new to her, after all.

She didn't see or sense the figure come up behind her, nor did she hear the click of the stiletto. But she did feel the searing pain in her back, and a second stab in her side that seemed so cruelly gratuitous, before the person grabbed her bag and fled.

Slowly, she slid down the girder, where she sat, eyes focusing on the red emergency button at a check point nearby, thinking if she could only pull herself together, she might reach it. But instead the young woman just fixed her eyes on that goal as blood and life oozed from her wounds; sat there, staring, staring, until the red circle blurred, followed by a darkness that lasted not long at all and forever.

1

The summer Sierra Kane turned eighteen, Keith, her foster father, tried to rape her.

The paunchy but muscular man in his thirties stumbled into her bedroom in the middle of the night, drunk, clumsily climbed onto the mattress, then fumbled around for her as if she were something he'd misplaced.

She would have been more frightened if his attempt hadn't seemed cartoonish — not that anything was ever funny about rape.

But Sierra had anticipated this unwanted attention – the signs had long been growing – and one swift knee to where it sent the most discouragement brought an abrupt and, judging by his reaction, appropriately painful close to an episode as unnecessary as it was unpleasant.

After all, the eighteen-year-old had months ago approached Molly, Keith's wife, who might well have done something in response to her charge's growing unease.

Sierra had told her, "I don't like the way 'Dad' has been staring at me." She had used air quotes to stress her point.

Peeling potatoes at the kitchen table, the round woman with

short graying brown hair barely glanced at her latest foster child. "And how's that?"

"Like he's the breadwinner and I'm dessert."

Her foster mother had a musical laugh that Sierra had once found endearing. "Oh, that's ridiculous, dear."

Sierra raised a single eyebrow. "You haven't noticed?"

Molly set the paring knife down. "Sierra. You've turned into such a beautiful young woman, it would be hard for any healthy man *not* to stare."

"Well, it feels *unhealthy* to me."

The foster mother's eyes finally met Sierra's. "I'll talk to Keith later...now help me with dinner."

Whether Molly had or hadn't spoken to her husband was now moot. Sierra had learned a long time ago when it was time to leave. Which was, in a way, a pity. She'd been with the middle-aged childless couple for three years — the longest time spent with any foster parents.

Through no real fault of her own, Sierra had been passed from family to family here in Omaha, due not to any bad behavior on her part, but the general corrosion of the traditional family unit — divorces, out-of-state job transfers, drugs, alcohol, mental illness. (All of that had been covered in Current Issues class.) Molly and Keith had been the most stable of a succession of caregivers, kind and considerate, but lately their marriage had hit choppy waters...Keith drinking too much most evenings, loud arguments behind closed doors.

Sierra would miss Molly, who had helped the girl legally change her name from "Candy," which she'd always detested. That sickening label had been courtesy of her real mother, as if abandoning the baby at birth hadn't been bad enough.

And hadn't it been Molly who took her shopping for clothes, showed her how to use make-up, and got the blossoming young woman on the pill? And hadn't Keith helped with homework, taught Sierra to drive, and bought her a cell phone?

She'd felt as comfortable and safe in Keith's presence as

Molly's...until his fatherly attention began to show signs of a not-so-hidden agenda.

Too bad. Over time, Sierra had grown to genuinely like the couple — love was way too strong a word — but she had long ago learned not to get attached to foster parents. This hadn't even been the first rape attempt, just the first one in this family. But, in the end, didn't they betray her like all the others?

Which made Sierra glad she hadn't shared with Molly and Keith something that happened at school, an opportunity she'd not quite come to terms with, even though she could have used some parental advice.

One gloomy overcast morning a month to the day before graduation night, high school guidance counselor Dolores Graham had summoned the student to her office.

Suddenly Sierra wondered if she didn't have enough credits to graduate, or if the counselor knew one of her teachers was going to give her a failing grade — perhaps in Algebra, where she was struggling.

The girl sat before the counselor's immaculately arranged desk awaiting pronouncement of her fate.

Mrs. Graham began, typically gruff: "You have plans for college?" Her face seemed etched with a permanent scowl – clearly, any idealistic aspirations that years ago might have led the woman into this job had long since eroded.

"Not really," Sierra said. "Well...community college, maybe."

The counselor picked up a thick white manilla envelope, tossed it across the desk to land in front of Sierra, dislodging a few loose papers that fluttered to the floor.

"What's this?" Sierra asked, gathering the stray sheets.

"A scholarship offer."

"I didn't apply for one anywhere."

"In this particular instance, your name was provided to a college recruiter."

"Why?"

Mrs. Graham obviously didn't like being on this end of an interrogation. "Because you met certain qualifications."

"Like what?"

The counselor tossed a hand. "It's all in there. Take it home, read it, decide."

Sierra picked up the packet, which bore an official-looking seal in the left upper corner, a large B in its center.

With a frown, Sierra asked, "What college is this?"

"Barnard. It's a very exclusive women's liberal arts school."

Sierra thought she might have heard of it. "Where's it located?"

A sigh. An eye roll. And finally a response: "Manhattan."

New York City! She'd never been there. A shiver of excitement coursed through her.

Mrs. Graham crisply said, "You should probably pursue it, as far as it goes. But it is unlikely to go *anywhere*, if you ask me."

Sierra stood, the envelope clutched to her chest like a life preserver, smiled, said, "I didn't ask you."

And left.

After school that day, sequestered in her bedroom, with Keith and Molly away at their respective jobs, Sierra opened the envelope and withdrew a folder. Inside, an official-looking letter greeted her.

"Congratulations! On behalf of the Committee on Admissions, I am very pleased to inform you that you have been admitted to Barnard College, pending your acceptance of the generous scholarship offered by the Mary Pearson Stafford Foundation."

The rest of the letter sang the canned praises of the venerable college, its esteemed accomplishments, its far-sighted policies — including a student diversity rate of forty percent — then ended with the flourishing signature of the director of admissions, Kim Ly.

A second letter from the foundation itself boiled down to this: the scholarship Sienna was being offered covered one year's tuition, plus room and board and all school fees.

If this was acceptable, she was to call the foundation's number (included) no later than July 30, to facilitate the transfer of funds to the college on her behalf. She was instructed to arrive on campus no sooner that August 29, using the enclosed student flexible fare, a one-way, open-ended ticket from Eppley Airfield to LaGuardia.

If it all sounded too good to be true – especially to an abandoned child with a C-plus average and no discernible special talents – a visit to the foundation's website via her cell quelled her qualms.

Mary Pearson Stafford had been a foundling (such an old-fashioned term!), an average student from Illinois. Stafford had attended Barnard in the fall of 1950 thanks to a patron who felt college should not be just for the wealthy and/or brilliant, and that many young women did not fully develop their intellectual potential until given an opportunity for higher learning.

Such was the case with Mary Pearson Stafford, who credited her success in business to her time at Barnard — even though she attended but a single year — which had led to her creating a scholarship foundation giving other Midwestern women, who'd faced life as orphans or foundlings, the same start.

Wikipedia confirmed the information, while offering more details, including the date of Stafford's birth and death (1930-1981) and the orphanage in Peoria where she lived (the Home for the Friendless — now called the Children's Home). Building her wealth in the international import and export trade, the never-married Stafford had been childless herself, though Gloria Steinem had called her, "the surrogate mother of so many successful young women." Stafford died at fifty-one while on a business trip to Paris.

The morning after the rape attempt, Sienna stayed in her bedroom waiting for Keith and Molly to go off to work. If they missed her at breakfast, they didn't stop at her door to express concern. When the two were safely gone, she packed only one suitcase — she was accustomed to leaving things behind — called for an Uber, then scrawled on the refrigerator message board:

Goodbye.
S

2

Sierra, arriving at LaGuardia in the early afternoon and stepping out onto the jet bridge into the concourse, was unprepared for the tumultuous tableau awaiting her. At Eppley, travelers seemed in no hurry, whichever end of the trip they were on – arriving in plenty of time for a flight, or in no hurry getting back home. Not here.

Following signs to baggage claim, she tried to find a slow lane, but there just wasn't one – no matter where Sierra maneuvered, she seemed in somebody's way. Soon she resigned herself to being swept along with the crowd, which fortunately flowed toward her destination.

Yet the baggage claim stations weren't crowded at all, most returning passengers toting carry-ons, heading routinely toward various ground transportation. When her one heavy bag finally came down the shoot, Sierra dragged it off the conveyor with some difficulty, then wheeled it over to a daunting map of the subway system.

A woman in black t-shirt and leotard, a duffle bag slung over one shoulder as if she were going straight from a plane to a fitness center, stopped to check the map.

Sierra asked her fellow traveler, "If I want to go Barnard College—"

The lady snorted. "If that's where you're going, take a cab – you can afford it." And moved on.

Sierra hated to admit defeat so early in the game, but she wanted out of this madhouse, and a ride directly to the college did sound calming. She peeled the sarcasm away from the woman-in-black's response and took the advice buried there.

But the cab driver, a beefy bald man with no neck and an unpronounceable name, immediately upon leaving the airport began speeding dangerously, weaving in and out of traffic, making her regret the first decision of her new life. Then, as they crossed the RFK Bridge, cars came to a near standstill. Just when Sierra might have been enjoying the iconic view of a looming Manhattan, she fixated upon the rising count of the meter, watching her modest but hard-earned savings from a summer job at the Pizza Palace dwindle.

Somewhere in this unfamiliar city, vaguely near the college, unable to stand the crawl any longer, she asked the cabbie to let her out. He shrugged sourly and pulled over. With her cell as navigation, Sierra trekked on, pulling the suitcase behind her, aware she was at times causing pedestrian congestion, garnering frowns that only deepened at her apologies, a practice she soon abandoned.

And the weather was so hot! There seemed to be no air circulating at all, tall buildings blocking any breeze, heedless of the tiny creatures below. While it could get plenty warm in Omaha, a wind always seemed to be blowing in from the flat plains.

By the time Sierra reached Barnard's main entrance on Broadway, she might have been caught out in a storm, so matted was her hair, her bright summery cotton clothes (so out of place here) clinging to her as if for dear life. Plus, her feet were as filthy as they were aching, the flimsy sandals no match for Manhattan's mean, grungy streets.

Opposite the busy boulevard was Columbia University, a crosswalk with meridian connecting the two colleges. Barnard was affiliated with the much larger Ivy League school – a little sister under her big brother's protection, a holdover from male-dominated days.

Only, their little sis — Sierra was about to find out — had grown up.

The black wrought-iron gates of Barnard stood yawning open, a small guard booth unattended, as if she were expected but not worth a welcome. She passed through an elaborately scrolled archway into a cobblestoned courtyard.

Straight ahead was Barnard Hall, a large four-story, red-brick Colonial-style structure with thick columns guarding the front doors; the imposing building likely dated to the college's inception, and in any case looked old, if well-preserved, a dowager who could afford plastic surgery.

This was not her destination, however; Sierra, who had memorized the map from her packet, was heading to Milbank Hall, the administrative building at the north end of the campus. She and her suitcase turned right to follow the brick walkway past modern Milstein Center, Altschul Hall and the Diana Center, stopping at the building at the end. Milbank mirrored Barnard Hall in its architecture, except for pillars supporting a second-floor balcony.

Milbank Hall was also larger, with U-shaped wings, and a lovely front courtyard with accent trees, carefully trimmed evergreen bushes, and old-fashioned lampposts. A welcoming breeze from the nearby Hudson River awaited her, which she fully appreciated in her uncomfortably damp condition.

Inside, she stood for several moments, taking in the interior splendor — cream-colored walls, high ceilings, marble-like flooring, with more columns arranged here and there to lend an improbable cozy atmosphere. She couldn't help feeling some semblance of reverence, thinking about the hundreds of young women who had passed through these portals with hopes and dreams of bettering their lives. And now she was one of them.

Of course, she immediately batted this sensation away. If Sierra had learned anything in her short life, it was to keep her expectations low.

The Office of Admissions was on the first floor, but the frosted-glass-and-wood door was locked. A bench beckoned nearby, and she settled herself there, suitcase tucked to one side, and waited. Someone would come along. After all, the building might look like a stone mausoleum, but it was infested with life, noises filtering down from upper floors — the slam of a door, shoes clacking on stairs, the echo of voices — the administrative staff gearing up for an influx of students.

An attractive Asian woman came into view – petite, slim, her sleek black hair shoulder-length. She wore a white silk shirt, red skirt, and multicolored trainers. One red-nailed hand carried a small brown sack, the other an iced drink in a clear plastic cup embossed with the words "The Hungarian Pastry Shop."

"Well, hello," she said, friendly.

"Hello."

"May I be of help?" A security badge hanging from her slender neck identified her as Kim Ly, Head of Admissions.

"I'm Sierra Kane. Freshman class."

The woman's smile lifted and so did her eyebrows. "Our new Stafford scholarship recipient." Her eyes went to the suitcase. "A little early, aren't you? Orientation isn't for another two weeks."

"I'm sorry. My situation was such that I, uh...just had to get away."

The administrator nodded slowly, as if understanding, despite the lack of specifics. "Well, please. Come on in."

As Kim Ly unlocked the doors, Sierra gathered her handbag and suitcase. She was then led through an outer area where metal office furniture clashed with ornate ceiling moldings, wall wainscoting, and a Victorian-era rug, a window air conditioner chugging valiantly like a referee between old and new. She followed the admissions head into the small matching office beyond.

While Kim Ly retreated behind her desk, Sierra took the chair in front.

"I know I'm early," Sierra began, "but couldn't I stay in the dorm?"

The arcs of the woman's dark hair swung. "That's not possible, I'm afraid. Campus security isn't up to speed as yet. Insurance concerns. And the dorms are being cleaned and in some instances painted."

"Oh. I understand."

The woman cocked her head. "Forgive my bluntness, but what shape are your funds in?"

"Strictly cash, frankly. And just a little over five hundred."

Red lips pursed. "Not enough to cover two weeks' rent anywhere." She studied Sierra for perhaps five seconds, which seemed much longer. "Tell you what – you could stay with me, if you like."

Sierra wondered if she'd heard the woman correctly. "With *you*? Really?"

Half a smile dimpled a cheek. "Can't have the Stafford scholarship winner camped out on the bench outside my door, can I?"

The woman sounded serious!

Sierra blurted, "Thank you – thank you *so* much."

Kim lifted a red-nailed finger. "Don't thank me just yet. I'll make good use of you. With three staff members out with summer flu, I could really use an extra pair of hands. Are you up for that?"

"I'd love to pitch in," Sierra replied, meaning it. Plus, it seemed like the right thing to say.

"Excellent. How are your computer skills?"

"Not bad."

"Good. I'll get you started scanning papers."

Sierra shifted in the chair. "Could I ask you something?"

"Of course."

"How many other Stafford scholarship students are enrolled at Barnard this year?"

Two fingers came up like a peace sign. "Just two. You, and last year's recipient, who'll be returning as a sophomore next week. You'll be dorm-mates, by the way."

"I understood the scholarship could extend a full four years, if I maintained a three-point average."

Kim Ly nodded. "That's true, but two years is the typical length any of the women have stayed."

"Why *is* that, if I might ask? The difficulty of maintaining a high enough grade point?"

A silk-shouldered shrug. "That has been the case, at times. In other instances, the women have gone on to scholarships at schools in their home states, while others pursue opportunities in business. A variety of reasons, but nothing that would define *your* experience, necessarily."

That made sense to Sierra, or at least enough sense for her to move on to the question she'd been asking herself since the day that congratulatory letter came.

She sat forward. "Do you know why they picked me? I mean, out of a field of candidates whose qualifications include *not* being outstanding?"

Kim Ly smiled at that. "Well, *someone* had to win."

"...Oh."

The admissions head must have known she'd sounded flip, because she leaned forward and her voice took on a just-between-the-two-of-us air.

"I don't mean to talk out of school, so to speak. But I do believe the foundation board mentioned, in our correspondence, liking that you'd changed your name. It used to be Candy, didn't it?"

That surprised Sierra. The woman knew that without looking at a file or anything. But that she'd changed her name hardly seemed worth bragging about.

"Yes," Sierra said. "I hated it."

"Good call. It demonstrated a desire to define yourself. Well, are you ready to start scanning papers?"

"I am."

She opened the small brown bag. "Cream puff?"

3

At a little after six that evening, a black Mercedes drew up in front of Barnard. Tall, mustached, in a dark suit, a chauffeur emerged, came around, opened the back door for Kim Ly and Sierra, closed them in, then wordlessly deposited Sierra's suitcase in the trunk.

He slid back behind the wheel and Kim Ly, seated behind him, said, "Jason...would you mind taking the scenic route?"

"Not at all, Ms. Ly," he replied with a British accent that Sierra found charming. She wondered if it were real.

The sedan pulled away from the curb and headed down Broadway.

Kim Ly's smile was barely there as the younger woman tried not to be too wide-eyed as they glided by marquees boasting the newest plays, including some not-so-new-ones (*The Lion King*, *Wicked*), the lights of Broadway glowing atmospherically in the dusk. Just beyond Times Square, the driver turned east on 44th, then south along 5th Avenue, passing by Grand Central Terminal, with the Chrysler and Empire State Buildings in view.

At East 20th Street, the car swung left and soon circled a secluded, foliage-filled park enclosed by a black wrought-iron spiked fence; the vehicle came to a stop on the corner of East 21st and Gramercy Park at a six-story white limestone with arched windows.

After depositing his fares and luggage on the sidewalk, the chauffeur asked, "Usual time tomorrow morning, Ms. Ly?"

"Yes. And I'll be having this young woman with me throughout the week."

He nodded and made an offer to carry Sierra's suitcase, but she politely declined.

As the driver returned to his car, Sierra turned to her hostess. "Thank you. That was lovely." Then, unable to help herself, added, "A girl could get used to that kind of thing."

Kim Ly's red lips formed a broader smile now. "Couldn't she just?"

Sierra followed the woman through a gate and up three steps to an archway with a carved wooden door, which Kim Ly unlocked. They entered into a cool vestibule.

"The building was gutted back in the eighties," her hostess said, "and made into four apartments.... This is me." She pointed to their left. "I was lucky to get it — and on the first floor, no less."

Her hostess unlocked the door, and Sierra and her suitcase entered a modern world of white — walls, carpet, furniture, drapes — punctuated only by a large framed picture over the white-bricked fireplace of a can of Campbells soup, the red of it startling against all that white. In one corner stood a black lacquered folding screen with dragons.

An open, banister-less staircase led to a mezzanine; from the entryway below, Sierra could glimpse a couch, modern desk and chair, and tall, wall-hugging bookcases.

"That's my office," Kim Ly said, "where you'll be sleeping."

"Are you sure you won't be needing it?"

"My laptop-in-bed will suffice." She went on, "My room is up another flight, as is the bathroom."

Sierra nodded.

"Oh, one other thing that may come in handy..." The admissions head pointed to a key on a hook. "I have access to the private park across the street, only available to people who live *on* the park. As my guest, you can have access to it, too." She waggled a red-nailed finger. "But don't lose that key. It's a bitch to replace."

"I won't." Sierra managed not to react, hearing the casual swear word coming from a Barnard administrator.

Kim Ly gestured with both hands. "Let's get you settled in."

IN THE FOLLOWING DAYS, on the drive to and from the college via the West Side Highway — a much shorter trip than the "scenic route" — Sierra learned quite a bit about Kim Ly.

In her late forties but looking a decade younger, she was a first-generation-born American whose parents had fled Vietnam after the fall of Saigon. Raised in San Diego, she'd graduated from the University of California in Berkeley with a doctorate in Education, going on to hold administrative positions at the University of Chicago and Penn State. Next stop: New York and a position at Barnard in the Office of Admissions, advancing to head the department. Some years ago she met, married, then divorced a Wall Street financier. They had no children.

Less forthcoming, Sierra divulged little about her past in these chats, offering morsels but never a meal, before steering the conversation back to the questioner.

They worked hard and well together, and dined out in the evenings, catching a film and a play and otherwise just sitting quietly, with Kim Ly telling her guest what she could expect in the coming classes.

On Friday, over coffee and scones at the white breakfast table, Kim Ly informed Sierra that student crew captains would be arriving on the weekend to help with NSOP (New Student Orientation Programs). This meant a dorm room could be made available then.

"You don't seem pleased to hear that," Kim Ly said, mildly surprised.

"Sorry. I guess I've been enjoying the high life too much."

Her hostess chuckled. "Everyone needs something to strive for."

She sipped coffee and smiled over the cup. "Don't worry, I'll have you back for dinner sometime — I make a mean Bun Cha."

Sierra didn't know what that was, or care. But she put some eagerness in as she said, "Promise?"

Kim Ly placed her slender, red-nailed hand over Sierra's, resting on the table. "Promise."

The gesture made Sierra uncomfortable, and she slowly withdrew her hand. There wasn't anything overtly sexual about it, really. The woman seemed genuinely nice, even warm at times. But was Kim Ly just someone else who wouldn't keep her word?

Sierra's memory replayed another "nice" woman's voice.

"Dear," Molly said, *"you have to stop holding people to such high standards. Everyone's human, even you – we all make mistakes."*

Like ignoring a husband who crawled into bed with a foster child?

Kim Ly was saying, "Listen...I'm caught up with work thanks to your help, so why don't you take the day off? Use my extra set of keys. Go to the park, wander around, just have a good time."

The park was a liberty she hadn't taken. "Are you sure?"

"Absolutely."

A horn beeped.

The woman rose. "That's Jason. I'll see you tonight."

After Kim Ly had departed, Sierra cleared the table, hand-washed the dishes, then gathered the spare house keys, along with the special one on the hook, and left.

Gramercy Park was story-book enchanting, the early morning sun dappling through the trees, leaves just starting to turn colors, shimmering in the breeze. Paths led to secluded areas where well-maintained flower beds complemented fountains and statues. She alone seemed to be enjoying the serenely soothing setting, which was a pity.

Of course, most of the city was at work now, and this idyllic spot was forbidden to tourists and all but a few select Manhattanites. Then the Midwestern girl, even if she was from big-city Omaha, remembered that New York was supposed to be dangerous.

Snow White in the forest, she wandered back to the edge of the park.

She selected a wrought-iron bench facing the sidewalk and just sat for a while, enjoying the solitude, watching pedestrians walk or jog by. Others paused to stare at her through the bars, people who looked like money seeming to wonder what a creature like her was doing in a private space. She felt like a monkey in a cage, if in an exclusive zoo. A man who did *not* look like money stopped and raised a middle finger and shook it at her, before moving on.

That's my cue, Sierra said to herself, and left the park.

For several hours she roamed, just taking it all in, and then had a thought: *Isn't the foundation's office somewhere around here?*

She ducked into a Starbuck's and, over a vanilla latte, consulted her phone. *Yes!* The address she'd entered from the Stafford Foundation letterhead was only a few blocks away – no room number, just "3rd Floor." But that would be enough.

She would take the opportunity to thank someone at the foundation in person for the generous scholarship, and assure whoever-it-was that she would seize this opportunity. With no hesitation at all, Sierra walked briskly to the corner of East 42nd Street and Madison Avenue, paused to look up at this latest impressive building, and went in.

In the lobby she approached a counter behind which a crisply uniformed woman was tending to a briefcase-lugging businessman. Their conversation seemed to involve a problem that might take time fixing, so Sierra moved on toward a bank of elevators.

She glanced around for a building directory, saw none and impulsively boarded an elevator and went up to the third floor, alone in the car. That struck her as odd – didn't all New York business buildings buzz with activity?

But no directory awaited her on three, either. Nor did any of the closed office doors list anything but numbers. And the hall was echoey and empty. An odd anonymity seemed to possess the place.

Then a sign of life: down the hallway came a tall, slender young man in tight black jeans, white shirt, thin silver tie, and gray suit-jacket. His short dark hair was sculpted into spikes. Casual Day?

"Excuse me," Sierra said, stepping in his path. "I'm looking for the Mary Pearson Stafford Foundation."

He put a hand on a hip and half a smirk on his face. "Did you check in downstairs?"

"No, the woman at Information was busy."

"Did you have an appointment today?"

"No. I just wanted to drop by and—"

"Then they probably aren't here."

He started off, but Sierra pressed: "But this *is* their address."

He looked back at her, the smirk shifting sides. "Theirs and a hundred other businesses."

Sierra frowned. "I don't understand."

He smiled patiently as if she were a backward child who simply had to be tolerated. "This floor is all virtual offices."

"Like...on a computer?"

"No! Rented out fully equipped! When needed? Hourly, daily, weekly, *whatever*?"

"Oh."

He turned toward her, his manner softening, taking mercy on this impossible bumpkin. "Saves money, *and* gives little companies a big Madison Avenue address. So unless you had a meet-and-greet set up..." He shrugged. "...you'll be talking to a desk and some empty chairs. That's *if* somebody lets you in."

And he moved on.

She retraced her steps to the bank of elevators, hopped another empty car, and returned to the lobby information counter, where the uniformed woman was no longer solving a problem.

"Uh...hello," Sierra began. "Excuse me. I thought I had a meeting on the third floor today."

As crisp as her uniform, she said, "Company?"

Sierra told the woman, who consulted her computer, and reported back: "I have nothing scheduled for them today."

"I might have mixed things up. Maybe it's *next* week."

Well-manicured fingers danced on the keyboard. "No, I'm sorry, and there's nothing scheduled after that." She studied the screen. "As a matter of fact, there's no record of that company using these offices in some time. They've lately only been having their mail picked weekly. You'd better contact them directly."

"Yes. I'll do that. Thank you. Sorry to bother."

"No trouble."

Sierra stood outside on the sidewalk, pedestrians rushing by as busy as the building she'd exited wasn't. Disturbed by the experience, she could only wonder if there was something shady about the foundation's arrangement.

On the other hand, why spend money on permanent office space when those funds could go toward more scholarships? It wasn't as if student applicants came to Manhattan knocking on their door.

Even if she just had.

Most of all, though, she was disappointed not to be able to thank some representative of her benefactors in person. No reason to think anything was amiss. Not at all suspicious. Move along. Nothing to see here.

Anyway, that's what Sierra told herself.

4

Brooks Hall sounded like a rich guy's name. Instead it was Sierra's designated dorm, one of four student housing facilities — along with Hewitt, Reid, and Sulzberger — arranged in a square with a central courtyard, a complex affectionately referred to as "the quad." Or not so affectionately by students who drew an un-air-conditioned hall, as she had.

Her room contained two single beds, two desks, and two wardrobes, each side mirroring the other. The furniture was ancient but sturdy, the floor's linoleum tiles old but polished, walls freshly repainted to cover the former occupancy's indiscretions. Sierra imagined that the hall hadn't changed much since Mary Pearson Stafford's day.

Nonetheless, everything in the dorm room was clean, drawers opened and closed, doors didn't come off their hinges. She'd lived in worse places.

Selecting the bed nearest the window, she hoisted her suitcase onto the bare mattress, woefully aware of how many essentials she still needed: bedding, towels, toiletries, to mention a few, which didn't include school supplies. At least she had her own laptop.

After storing her clothes in the wardrobe, Sierra left to drop in on Kim Ly.

She found the reception area's desk still unattended and the inner-office door open, revealing the admissions head behind her desk, on the phone, in a rather incensed state, some poor lackey on the other end the recipient of considerable ire.

Sierra, frozen in the doorway, had never seen this side of Kim Ly before, and started to back away.

Noticing her, the woman waved the student forward, ending the call with, "Just do it!"

"I can, uh, come back later," Sierra said.

"No, please," Kim Ly responded pleasantly. "Have a seat."

Sierra sat. "Ummm...I was just wondering...what does Barnard do with things students leave behind?"

"Need something?"

Sierra smiled embarrassedly. "Just pretty much everything."

The administrator's eyebrows lifted; so did the corners of her mouth. "We keep a storage room in the basement, where items are held for a while before being donated." She paused. "You'd be welcome to anything you find."

"That'd be great."

The woman cocked her head. "But you do need to think about getting a job."

Leaning forward, Sierra asked, "Is there any possibility I could stay on here, helping out in the office?"

"I'm afraid not. My assistants will be back tomorrow. And I rather thought your room and board at my place made a fair trade for the work you put in here in their absence."

"Oh, absolutely."

Kim Ly frowned in thought. "Didn't you mention you've worked as a waitress?"

"Yes." She hadn't really considered that option, however, having heard how rude New Yorkers could be, especially to wait staff. Tending tables would be a lot harder here than at a Midwestern pizza joint.

The administrator was saying, "We have arrangements with several restaurants, and I can contact them for you."

"If it's not too much trouble." Her savings of five hundred dollars would dwindle soon enough.

"I'll get right on that," Kim Ly said, and made a note. The harsh woman on the phone was nowhere to be seen. "I forgot to ask you this morning – how was your day off? Did you enjoy the park?"

"Very much." Sierra reported enthusiastically about her time there, minus the middle-finger salute.

But she did tell the woman about the impromptu visit to the Madison Avenue address of the Stafford Foundation, which appeared to serve only as a mail pick-up.

"I'm not surprised," Kim Ly said, then validated the conclusion Sierra had come to. "Stafford's not really the type of organization that needs an office in the city."

Head cocked, Sierra asked, "Have you ever met with anyone from the foundation?"

"Only by phone." She frowned. "Why? Is that a concern somehow?"

Not anxious to strain their relationship, Sierra replied quickly, "Oh, no reason. It just seemed a little mysterious at first. And I was disappointed I couldn't tell someone in person how grateful I am. I suppose a letter would be as good."

"*Better*, actually. And I'd suggest waiting until you've been here a while, so you can write about your courses and your experiences." The desk phone trilled. "Sorry, I've got to take this...."

Sierra rose. "Of course. Thanks for seeing me." Phone receiver in hand, the administrator said, "Any time."

Soon, finding the door to the basement unlocked, Sierra descended brick steps into a dank, stuffy concrete chamber. Adding to the claustrophobic atmosphere was a low ceiling and narrow hallways seeming to lead in all directions.

But a diagram posted on a nearby wall to the right of where the stairs came out told her where she could find the storage room. She followed the directions dutifully, feeling like a mouse in a maze sniffing the prize ahead. Then she rounded a hall corner and stopped short at an actual dead rat in a cheese-baited trap. Shuddering, she hurried on.

Surprisingly, the storage room had quite an extensive array of items stacked on metal shelves — or perhaps not so surprisingly, considering the disposable income Barnard students had (or rather, their parents did). After all, what was it to them, replacing, say, a power strip?

Sierra found a plastic laundry basket – checking off one item from her mental list – and then began filling it with anything she thought might come in handy, including, yes, a power strip. Also a pair of shower shoes (if somewhat too big), laundry detergent, pens and notebooks, an *I ♥ Barnard* coffee mug, and even a small fan.

Just like shopping at Goodwill, only even cheaper – prices didn't get any better than free!

Her basket brimming, Sierra was about to leave when she spotted an overlooked book bag: large, black, with lots of zippered compartments, and covered with sewn-on anime patches and video game pins. Some of the adornments she recognized – characters in *JoJo's Bizarre Adventure*, avatars from games like *Final Fantasy* and *Sims 3*. While Sierra wasn't much into that kind of stuff – a guy she'd dated briefly had been – she could really use a backpack, and the patches and pins could always be removed.

Except for one that made her smile: the San Diego Comicon logo. That was the epicenter of cosplay, which was one thing she knew all about. She liked to play characters of her own design, which let her be whoever anyone wanted her to be. At Elkhorn High she was a floater, fitting in with geeks and gamers, fine-arts and jocks. Making lots of friends, but no close ones.

On her way back through the maze, Sierra passed a door-less room filled with metal filing cabinets, and drifted in with her basket, still shopping. Maybe there was something here she could use....

Cabinet drawers were labeled by years going back decades, and she pulled one open at random. Expecting old dusty files, she found instead small boxes identified as microfilm, neatly arranged, as were flat square envelopes holding microfiche (she'd used both at the Omaha Public Library).

She was about to close the drawer when it occurred to her that these records might include Mary Pearson Stafford. Could be interesting to see what courses her benefactor had taken — certainly nothing currently offered in the Women's, Gender, and Sexuality Studies program! — and maybe even what kind of grades she got. Who was this woman from the past who was impacting Sierra's present...and future?

Fueled by curiosity, Sierra located the drawer marked 1950, the year the Stafford woman had attended Barnard, set down her basket, and opened the drawer. Thumbing through the microfiche envelopes, she stopped at one labeled STUDENT ROSTER.

Sierra would need a microfiche reader to access the information, but the college library should have one. She tucked the envelope in the basket with her other appropriations, then headed out of this nest of file cabinets.

A middle-aged man in work-clothes lurched into her path, blocking the way. Where he'd come from, she could not say, but Sierra nearly dropped the basket. After all, even with permission, her plundering seemed sketchy at best.

"What are you doing in here?" he asked gruffly. An ID on a lanyard designated him as a custodian.

Sierra replied, "Ms. Ly with Admissions said I could have anything from the student storage room."

He pointed a filthy finger behind her. "Well, that doesn't include in *there!* That's private administrative storage."

"I must have taken a wrong turn."

He hovered menacingly. "Damn right you did – *this* area is off-limits...'specially to students."

"Yes, sir," Sierra said, more meekly than she felt. Then, helpful but not really, she said, "There's a rat in a trap back there." She nodded in that direction. "You might want to tend to that."

She thought he might take that as the dig it was, but his face lit up like a kid Christmas morning. "Ah! Finally *snared* the little bugger!"

"Not so little," she pointed out.

But he had already turned and was disappearing into the maze.

Back in the dorm room, Sierra was unloading the basket onto the mattress when the door opened and a young Black woman entered – tall, lithe, with flawless copper skin, braided hair twisted into a bun at the nape of her neck, so stunning she might have been a model.

"Tiara Williams," she announced and held out a fist.

"Sierra Kane." Sierra fist-bumped and gestured to the bed. "I'm not laying claim or anything. You can have this side if you like."

Tiara shrugged. "Doesn't matter. Besides, I won't be here that long."

"Quitting school before it starts?"

The smile came easy. "No, honey. I've signed a lease on a place in Harlem. But it'll be a while before I can move in." She paused. "Where you from?"

"Omaha."

Tiara pointed to herself with a long red nail. "Chicago. My foster parents live in the projects. Cabrini Green?"

Sierra hadn't heard of it.

"You don't get around, do you? Cabrini used to be pretty notorious, but they're refurbishing things. Bet you wish Barnard would refurbish *this* dump."

"It's not so bad."

The roommate didn't argue the point. "Anyway, you'll have this space all to yourself soon enough. I doubt they'll assign anyone else to you."

Sierra blinked. "What is this, quarantine?"

Tiara corrected herself. "I mean, there aren't any other *Stafford* girls besides you and me, and they like to keep us together."

So, quarantine.

The roommate's eyes drifted to the items on the mattress and stayed there. "Where did you get that backpack? Wardrobe?"

"No, in the storage room in Milbank Hall. Stuff abandoned by students." Sierra gestured to the array of things she'd emptied from the basket, including the backpack. "Why? Do you know who it belonged to?"

"Sure do. Emily Stewart."

"Do you think she'll want it back?"

"Not hardly."

Sierra waited for an explanation.

Tiara sighed. "She'd dead, honey."

Though obviously she hadn't known the woman, this news alarmed Sierra – that was the dead Emily Stewart's backpack, right there!

"What...what happened?"

"Got herself stabbed in the subway when someone snatched her purse."

Sierra's eyes remained glued like two more items on the black bag with its carefully applied patches and strategically placed pins.

The alarm faded. Oh, well. At one foster home, when she was in elementary school, Sierra once had to wear a dead girl's clothes, and this was just a backpack.

Tiara's eyes were on the decorated black bag, too. "Another Stafford girl," she said absently.

Sierra stared at her new roommate. "Is that why you thought the backpack was already in here somewhere? This was *her* room? And yours?"

Tiara nodded. "That's her bed you took. You want to trade?"

"No," Sierra said with a shrug.

The dead girl whose clothes she'd had to wear? Sierra had slept in her bed, too.

5

For Sierra, orientation week was a blur: obtaining an ID card, connecting her laptop to the campus network, tours of Barnard and Columbia, learning about dozens of resources available to students, lectures on getting along with roommates and professors, and how new students could become involved in college activities. Barnard seemed determined that every woman should succeed, no matter her interests or needs.

About the only time Sierra had free all week – lunches, dinners and evening entertainment were scheduled events – came during the college president's welcome to student families and friends, of which she had none, and so hadn't attended.

The busy week continued with sightseeing trips in the city and surrounding boroughs – Sierra obtaining a subway MetroCard – and the opportunity to see a Broadway show (*Wicked*), which Sierra skipped to save money. Anyway, Kim Ly had already taken her to more interesting Broadway fare (*Come From Away*).

Orientation wrapped up with a carnival, capped by an LGBTQ+ mixer; she attended the former, but made no effort to connect with anybody. Flying under the radar was her way, particularly at the start of any new phase of her existence.

When Monday arrived, so did a grind of classes with the expected prerequisites but also a required seminar; she had selected "Dead and Undead," which looked at horror movies and folklore and so on. For her Phys Ed class, keeping the sad demise of her backpack's former owner in mind, Sierra opted for Self-Defense.

Saturday morning, before the sun came up, she rolled out of bed for her first day at Big Apple Bites, a diner on Amsterdam, where Kim Ly had secured for her a twelve-hour stint every weekend.

Sierra was supposed to shadow another waitress, but – when the woman didn't show up – found herself on her own. Unprepared for the crush of customers, and the level of din and rudeness, she nonetheless persevered.

What got her fired her first day was an exchange with a man in a business suit who'd insisted on a four-person booth, despite the line of customers outside, then brusquely brushed off her offer to take his breakfast order as he studied his menu like a Sanskrit stone. Realizing table turnover was a priority, she tried again five minutes later.

After a second rude rebuff, Sierra said sweetly, "I'll just wait for a telepathic communication from you, shall I?" But probably it was her muttered, "Asshole," that lost her the job, after the man complained loudly to manager/owner, Grigor Hakobi.

Hakobi – a small, dark-haired, dark-eyed calm within the diner's perpetual storm – waited until Sierra finished her shift before summoning her to a tiny, messy backroom office that seemed to betray inner turmoil.

"I'm sorry," he said with a thick accent and sad eyes. "You are okay, a very efficient young lady. But you do not have the *kharnvatsk*..." He searched for the English equivalent. "...*temperament* for job."

"You mean for handling the abuse."

The man sighed, the world on his hunched shoulders. "Really, most customers are...pleasant."

"I was supposed to just be shadowing today. It won't happen again."

Hakobi shook his head, woefully. "That man, he is a regular, and important. If he saw you here...? There is no 'again,' I'm afraid."

She nodded.

He opened a drawer, brought out a black metal box, and removed some bills. "This should cover time and tips." His hand returned to the box and selected another.

"And this," he said with a small smile, "is for saying to him... 'asshole.'"

She accepted the money. "Thank you." Then, as an afterthought, "If you, uh, speak to Ms. Ly about my dismissal—"

"You had scheduling problem with classes, I say."

She gave him a similarly small smile, nodded, and left.

WHEN SIERRA RETURNED to her dorm room in the early evening, Tiara had moved out, leaving a note behind. The now ex-roommate explained she'd been able to take possession of the condo sooner than expected, listing the address. A postscript invited Sierra to a party the next night at her new digs.

Sunday morning Sierra slept in. Around noon, she showered and, because the weather had suddenly turned cool, slipped into jeans, a Barnard sweatshirt, and Keds. She collected the backpack, made her way out of the dorm, then crossed Broadway to Columbia University.

Butler Library was situated at the south end of the campus, butting up against West 114th Street. The massive rectangular limestone structure – built nearly a century ago in a typically Neoclassical style – boasted on its ten-story face a five-story row of twelve huge Corinthian columns.

Oddly enough, the grandiose exterior offered only a single entrance door, creating a bottleneck of coming and going students, making them a captive audience to a dozen or so sign-carrying, chanting females protesting the all-white-male writers — Aristotle, Homer, Plato, et al. — whose names where chiseled across the length of the facade.

As Sierra squeezed through, someone behind her stepped on her heel, causing a white tennis shoe to come off.

Inside, she hopped one-footed out of the way as best she could, turning in irritation, her ire quickly fading as she faced a sandy-haired young man wearing a light-blue Columbia rugby shirt, its color matching his eyes.

"My bad," he said sheepishly, Ked in one hand.

With a mischievous smile, he dropped to one knee, Prince Charming-style, to slide the shoe on her foot like a glass slipper, as irked students rounded this roadblock. No Cinderella, Sierra wasn't sure whether she was charmed or annoyed. There certainly weren't any singing birds.

She gave him a smirky smile and left him behind, moving through a checkpoint that accepted Barnard ID cards, then briefly stopped to consult a library directory before taking the stairs to the fourth floor.

The Periodicals and Microforms Reading Room — with its white and black diamond floor tiling and rows upon rows of wooden shelves for storing media — smelled of old newspapers and magazines. It was a familiar, comforting scent. She liked libraries.

In an area set aside for microform-reading machines, Sierra selected a booth, and sat. Then, from her backpack, she retrieved the microfiche, withdrew the film from its protective sleeve, and placed it beneath the viewing glass.

But no matter what adjustment tools she tried — enhance, zoom, contrast — the screen remained murky and splotched.

Someone tapped her on the shoulder.

She twisted in the chair.

The Keds snatcher held up a palm. "Not stalking you," he said. "This fell off your bag."

He placed an enamel Pikachu pin on the table next to the microfiche sleeve.

Putting no inflection into it, she said, "Thank you," and returned to the viewer.

But he was still there, his arm coming past her shoulder so he could point at the microform screen. "You won't get anything off of that."

"Why not?"

"It's oxidized."

"What's that mean?"

"The film contains a silver-gelatin emulsion that breaks down over time, or, you know, if not stored properly."

"It looks like it has the measles."

"Doesn't it?"

"Well...thanks," she said.

"See you around."

His inflection made that almost a question, but she didn't answer it.

When a glance confirmed her slipper bearer had moved on, Sierra removed the diseased fiche from beneath the glass and returned it to the sleeve, realizing he'd probably seen its label.

But then, what would a Barnard roster list from 1950 mean to some random Columbia guy, anyway?

6

Sunday evening, around nine, Sierra threw on a Barnard sweatshirt, jeans and some block-heel sandals, and – avoiding a thirty-minute trek, according to her cell's GPS – took a taxi to the party. She wasn't sure if walking alone in Harlem was wise.

But the cab ride along Martin Luther King Boulevard – with its stretch of upscale shops, restaurants, and entertainment venues (including the Apollo Theater) – convinced her she'd be able to hoof it safely back. The jog north into a tony section of Malcolm X Boulevard served to embarrass her for thinking otherwise.

She'd formed no expectation of what her ex-roommate's new digs might be like, but if she had, what the cab pulled up in front of wouldn't have been it: a large modern brick building with multi-level roof gardens, and a supermarket conveniently located on the ground floor. No wonder Tiara had left Brooks Hall behind.

The entrance for the condos was around the corner on West 129th Street, beneath a green canopy reading The Lenox Grand, right next to underground parking. Talk about having it all!

In the vestibule, she found Tiara's name on the intercom directory and soon was buzzed through. She took the elevator to the fifth floor, where a cream-color hallway with chocolate doors awaited.

Outside the apartment, hip-hop music bled through, requiring a loud knock.

The owner herself answered.

"You made it!" Tiara said, dressed in a slinky black silk top and leggings. Sierra immediately felt under-dressed for the promised casual party. "Come in!"

Tiara led Sierra down a gleaming wood floor, through a narrow vestibule, then into a large living area sparsely decorated with expensive contemporary furniture, new-leather smell battling the skunky scent of marijuana.

"Movers are bringing the rest tomorrow," Tiara explained with a dismissive wave. She shouted over the music, "Hey everyone! This is Sierra!"

Her dozen Black friends — some doing lines on a glass coffee table, others gathered around a card table temporarily posing as a liquor cart — barely acknowledged the newcomer. A white couple smoking weed on a couch gave her a bleary smile.

"I really made a hit," Sierra said.

"They made plenty of hits tonight already, honey." Tiara took her arm. "Come on...help me with the food."

In a modern kitchen off the living area, Sierra stood at a marble counter and stuffed large olives with a cheese mixture while Tiara fried chicken wings in a skillet.

Sierra asked, "What's this place set you back?"

"Three grand a month."

Sierra's mouth opened but no words came out.

Tiara shrugged. "I can afford it."

"Or do you mean there's a 'he' who can afford it?"

Her hostess waved that off. "No, no, no...I don't have a sugar daddy," she said. "My job can cover it."

"Your job. Which is...?"

Her friend transferred crispy wings onto to a paper towel, which either took concentration or simply indicated she was stalling before answering. Finally she turned to Sierra.

"I work for someone who deals in NFTs. Non-Fungible Tokens?"

Sierra had read an article about those. Something about getting an invisible wallet with magical money you dipped into to buy a minted token that came with a gas tax, and then you could park your NFT content in cold storage in an underground bunker. As if it were a flashy expensive sports car and not a bunch of zeros and ones.

Tiara was saying, "My employer does a lot of crypto, buying NFTs, and then selling them for a higher price."

Sierra nibbled one of the olives, then asked, "But what is it you *do*?"

Her friend flipped a hand. "I'm a courier. Before something is going to be listed in a certain marketplace, I pass the information along, so my employer can buy it first."

"Is that legal?" Sierra asked.

"Absolutely. It's not like insider trading on the stock exchange or anything. NFTs aren't regulated." She paused. "Think of it this way: let's say I work in the designer shoe department at Saks, and I get wind Louboutins are going on sale on such and such a day. And, as your friend who knows you love Louboutins, I give you a heads up. What's illegal about that?"

"Nothing." Actually, Sierra did love Louboutins, although she couldn't afford them, even on sale.

Tiara shrugged, drizzling buffalo sauce onto the wings. "Well, then."

"I don't suppose you could get *me* on the payroll," Sierra said, only half-joking.

Tiara shrugged. "Maybe."

"Really?"

"Doesn't hurt to ask."

Sierra stayed at the party until midnight, then walked back to her dorm, buoyed by the possibility of a lucrative job like Tiara's, and a little high on a line of cocaine.

The following week, Sierra fell into a pattern of going to Columbia's Butler Library after her last afternoon class, and doing the assignments in one of the many so-called "stacks," or study areas, central to every floor. The most popular was on the second, giving rise to the quest known as the Great Butler Seat Search; but in the late afternoon, it wasn't that difficult to find a chair at one of the forty-two rectangular tables for six.

The cavernous chamber, with its high, stained-glass ceiling, tall, iron-and-lead windows, and rich dark woodwork, wasn't as majestic (or gloomy, for that matter) as the library at Hogwarts, but impressive enough. She wouldn't have minded running into that guy who'd helped her out of, and back into, her Keds the other day, if only to put a name to him; but either he preferred another stack, or did his classwork elsewhere.

Toward the end of the week, however, Sierra came upon him hunkered over a fat textbook at a table, and found a place a few chairs down and opposite, from which she could surreptitiously study him. He had nice features and the sandy hair and blue eyes were pluses; older, maybe a senior or even a graduate student.

She was working on an excuse to approach him when another apparent older student, a slender and pretty female in a sorority-insignia sweatshirt, came up to him. A stiff conversation swiftly turned into an argument, ending abruptly in a *slap* across his face. It echoed like a gunshot.

The woman angrily departed in one direction, and he, after shoving the book into a backpack, rose and took off in the other.

What was that about? Sierra thought. *Maybe I'm better off not approaching him....*

But curiosity got the better of her, and Sierra followed the Keds guy out of the library exit onto West 114th Street, trailing some distance behind. Finally he went into a bar on Broadway.

After a few seconds, she steeled herself and entered the boxcar-style establishment, a long counter to the left, tables to the right, most of the lighting coming from glowing beer signs – the kind of place customers come to for liquor, not ambiance.

He was at the counter, in the center, hunched over what appeared to be whiskey in a tumbler.

Sierra sat, putting a stool between them.

The bearded middle-aged bartender, whose hard eyes had seen it all, said gruffly to her, "ID?"

"Diet Coke."

The young man noticed her. "Hey, Cinderella."

Cocking an eyebrow, she said, "You mind if I don't call you Prince Charming?"

He smirked. "I'm not so charming, it turns out. You were there, weren't you? At my table?"

"Yeah."

"And here I thought slapping guys went out of style."

"Apparently not." She moved over next to him, and stuck out a hand. "Sierra Kane."

He took and shook it. "Ethan Mitchell."

The bartender delivered her Diet Coke without enthusiasm.

"So you're at Barnard," Ethan said. "I noticed the sweatshirt the other day."

"Freshman. And you?"

"Senior...*still* a senior, I should say. Guess it's what they call taking a victory lap." He tossed down the remainder of the brown liquid. "I've been asked to pack my things and leave some of the finest institutions of higher learning in the nation."

"Really."

He nodded. "Cal State, Northwestern, Purdue. Columbia is my last chance, according to the Colonel."

"Who?"

"My father."

"He's a colonel? As in the military?"

"As in Colonel Sanders."

She frowned at him. "Your father owns a Kentucky Fried Chicken franchise?"

"Hell no. He owns an auto dealership in Kentucky. Colonel was an honorary title granted by the governor — just like Harland

Sanders was, back when it meant something. Nowadays the organization hands it out to just about anyone who'll give them money."

The bartender asked Ethan, "Another?"

"No thanks...I better go." He paid his bill with cash, along with Sierra's.

"Thank you," she said.

He stood. "You're welcome." He hesitated. "Listen, uh...I've got these two tickets to see *Six*, next Friday...."

Sierra had heard of the modern musical about the six wives of Henry VIII. The new ex who'd slapped Ethan had probably talked him into it.

"Anyway," he continued, "would you like to go? I mean, it's not a date, really."

"Sure," she said.

"I don't want to waste the ticket, and you might enjoy it. *Six*, I mean."

"I understand."

"Okay. Give me your number and I'll text you the information."

Sierra did, and he slipped out, awkward, embarrassed. Endearing. She finished the glass of soda, smiling to herself.

Walking back to Brooks Hall, her cell pinged.

But the message was from Tiara, not Ethan.

Got U an interview with my employer. B at my condo this Sat 8am.

7

Saturday morning, Sierra selected the most professional outfit she could assemble from her limited wardrobe – black tailored slacks, white silk blouse, black-and-white herringbone jacket with gold buttons – and set out for Tiara's condo, arriving fifteen minutes before the eight o'clock interview.

But when her friend answered the door with tangled hair and smeared make-up, wrapped up in a robe, Sierra's stomach dropped. Had she screwed up already?

Tiara read her face. "No, no, sweetie, you're on time...come in."

The living area bore remnants of another late-night party, frozen at the moment the lights were turned off. She glimpsed, down the hallway to her left, the backside of a nude Black man padding into the bathroom.

Sierra followed Tiara into the kitchen. "I don't understand."

"You will," the woman replied.

From the counter Tiara picked up a slender black cell phone. "You'll use this today....."

Confused, Sierra took it. "But...what about my interview?"

Tiara placed both hands on Sierra's shoulders and met her gaze patiently. "Honey, what you do today *is* the interview....Now listen carefully...."

With Tiara's instructions cemented in her mind, Sierra left the apartment and – using the Uber app on her new mobile, an account already set up in her name – summoned a ride.

Shortly, Sierra was picked up in front of the Lenox Grand and driven to Penn Station, where in Moynihan Train Hall she entered a Duane Reade convenience store. There, using a cell app from Bounce (a luggage storage network), she gave a confirmation number to the clerk, who disappeared into the back of the store, then returned with a soft black leather zippered briefcase-style bag, which Sierra signed for.

Inside the bag (as Tiara had said) Sierra found a round-trip train ticket from New York to Washington DC, a manilla envelope with cash, and a small sealed white envelope. The first two items she transferred to her purse; the last was to be delivered to a room at the Willard International Hotel, its seal intact.

With little time to spare – *Is all of this a test, substituting for an interview?* she wondered – Sierra caught the 9:05 Acela Express going to Union Station.

The ticket was first class for a solo window seat, complete with footrest and a little stationary table, the amenities mirroring a first-class airline cabin. An attendant – a female in a blue suit with red blouse – brought beverages and a snack box at Sierra's request, a bathroom only steps away.

The other passengers in the car, here and there, were mostly men. A section across from Sierra consisted of four seats — two forward, two backward — with a table, perfect for four-handed card games. Only one person occupied that space, however: a man in a dark gray suit in the backward aisle seat, *The Wall Street Journal* obscuring his face.

The train began to move, picking up speed, the city blurring away. Had Sierra known about the three-hour trip, she would have brought along her studies; as it was, she was left with her thoughts.

When the train settled into a rhythm, she began to get paranoid about the passenger across the way, who had either finished, or tired of, his newspaper, and now sat staring behind wire-rimmed glasses. All but facing each other made it impossible for her not to see him, or him her.

Had he not been there, she might have explored her new phone – what other apps she'd never heard of were waiting for her there? – or examined the briefcase at her feet, perhaps surreptitiously counting the money, or trying to determine what *exactly* was inside the sealed white envelope — *A piece of paper? A flash drive?* – without opening it.

But Sierra, convinced the man across the way was there to surveil her, did none of those things; she had no intention of failing at what she more and more believed was an audition, or possibly a dry run.

So she allowed herself to doze, but not deeply, waking up at each of the train's scheduled stops, and then drifting off again. And each time that passenger across the aisle was still there, feeding her suspicions.

Perhaps her fellow passenger was a competitor of the unknown NFT dealer, a rival who'd learned Sierra possessed important information for a buy, waiting for an opportunity to grab the briefcase, when she used the bathroom, say. Or maybe the right moment to grab the zippered bag as she moved in and out of sleep, straddling wariness and paranoia.

Then when the man disembarked in Baltimore — twenty minutes from DC — she felt foolish. Still, hadn't he been with her for most of the way? Long enough to report on Sierra to her would-be employer?

At Union Station, the briefcase firmly in hand, Sierra summoned another Uber for what turned out to be a short ten-minute ride to the Willard Hotel on Pennsylvania Avenue.

Mere blocks from the White House, the Willard was a monolithic twelve-story complex of several structures shuffled together, whose top floor had round protruding windows like bulging, unblinking eyes staring out skeptically over the nation's capital.

Inside, as instructed, Sierra bypassed the check-in desk, going straight to the bank of elevators that would take her to the sixth floor.

The ride up, in mixed company, unsettled her somewhat. The train ride had seemed oddly surreal. This felt too real.

She was shaking, just a little, as she knocked on the appropriate door, not knowing what to expect — or what she might be getting into.

But the silver-haired middle-aged man who answered put her immediately at ease. Handsome in a nicely craggy way, he might have been an actor past his prime yet still in demand, moving from leading man to character actor.

"Ah...Sierra, isn't it?" he said, radiating charisma and artificial warmth. "Right on time."

He led her into an elegantly anonymous suite whose decor was gray: walls, curtains, furniture, carpet.

"How was the train ride?" he asked.

"Very nice, thank you."

"I travel by rail whenever it's feasible – such a nice nostalgic change from these hectic airports, delayed flights, surly passengers. Don't you agree?"

"Oh yes," she said. As if she were an experienced traveler.

Her host's eyes went to the small zippered briefcase at her side. His smile was charming, though his tone was all business now, small talk over. "I'll take that, please."

She handed the bag with the white envelope to him. He twitched another smile, nodded, and disappeared into the adjoining bedroom, shutting the door, leaving her standing.

Was he checking its contents? Making sure the envelope hadn't been opened?

Her armpits felt moist, yet the air conditioning in here made it almost chilly.

Then he returned, with another disarming smile, gesturing to the gray couch. "Please, have a seat."

She took one end, he the other.

"Tell me," he began, "are you enjoying Barnard?"

Back to small talk. Tiara would have told him she was a freshman there. "Very much so."

"Good to hear. Have you given any thought to your area of study?"

Was he testing her? Or maybe *this* was the interview. If so, anything in the technical realm — say computer science — wouldn't be welcomed. Better she not know the difference between an NFT and the NFL.

With a smile of her own, Sierra replied, "I've been thinking of majoring in nineteenth-century French poetry."

Either he hadn't seen the movie *Groundhog Day*, or the reference had sailed over his silver-haired head; but in any case, his smile said he liked the answer. And she'd taken a year of French in high school, if barely passing.

He asked, "When does your train leave?"

"Three-thirty."

Her host patted his thighs. "I have to leave now, but you're welcome to stay. Order some lunch and charge it to the room."

She *was* hungry.

He stood.

She looked up at him. "I have a question, before you go."

"Please."

"Was this an audition of sorts? Or a one-time, uh, service you required? I understood this might lead to something...regular?"

Half a smile this time. "A job that might last the school year, at least? Oh, you have the position, Ms. Kane."

That he knew her last name was at once reassuring and unsettling.

"Thank you," she said. "Very much."

"And you're very welcome."

He was about to go when she risked another question. "Will I be making the same trip each time?"

"For now."

"How often?"

"As needed. With luck you won't miss many, perhaps not any, classes. The phone you were provided? Check it every morning and again at midnight."

Sierra stood and faced him; having him loom like that emphasized her subservience a little too much.

"Should that cell be used only when I'm working?"

He gestured vaguely. "Not at all...think of it as a perk."

That was good, because her cell was still in her foster father's name and he might cancel it at any time. She had other questions, but pressing further might jeopardize her employment, and Tiara could answer the rest.

He went back into the bedroom and returned with a zippered bag of his own, laptop-style.

"Excuse me," she said. "You know my name but I don't know yours."

He granted her one more smile. "'Mr. Jones' will have to do."

She nodded and watched him go, wondering if he was some lucky girl's father. Or something.

An hour later, after a delicious cobb salad, Sierra left the suite, somewhat reluctantly, although all that gray was a little much. In the elevator, just as the doors began to close, a female voice called out, "Hold it, please!"

Sierra pressed the "open" door button, and an attractive redhaired woman entered, wearing perfume that whispered and designer fashions that shouted.

She appeared to be in her mid-thirties — or well-preserved forties — her hair up in a French twist, her Gucci bag costing more than Sierra's entire wardrobe. Lots more.

"Thank you," the woman said.

"What floor?" Sierra asked, standing at the buttons like an old-time elevator operator.

"Fourth, please."

They took the quick trip in silence, and as the woman got off, she said, "You're a polite young woman."

"Thank you," Sierra said.

Then the Chanel No.5 and Gucci bag and the rest of it were gone, leaving the Barnard girl to wonder why that compliment had sounded like an insult.

Seemed like even her best clothes weren't good enough to pass muster at the Willard. But now she had some money to upgrade her look.

She'd already decided to open an account at the Citibank branch four blocks south from Barnard; the bank had an ATM on campus. She had her first deposit to make, and then a withdrawal to upgrade her business-trip look.

THE RETURN on the express was uneventful, and Sierra used the time to transfer information from her own cell to this new device, although she would continue to use hers for a while, as it was tied to the college network. And, also, it represented the only way Ethan had to get in touch with her for now.

She arrived back at Tiara's condo in the early evening.

"How did it go?" her friend asked, ushering her in.

"Fine."

They stood in the mouth of the living area, which had been tidied. "So did you make the grade?" Tiara asked.

"It appears so."

"Good."

"The man who met me...."

Tiara's eyes narrowed. "What did he look like?"

She thought for a moment. "The James Bond before Daniel Craig."

That made Tiara smile. "Call himself Mr. Jones?"

"Yes."

"That's the same dude I dealt with. Smooth."

"Is he the NFT dealer who hired you?"

"Probably not. Likely another go-between."

That surprised Sierra. "So you've never met your — *our* — employer?"

"Not that I know of."

"Do you even know his name?"

Tiara shook her head. "Honey, I don't ask questions. I do what I'm told, and take the money." She paused. "And you'd be wise to do the same. What's that old expression? Don't look a gift horse in the mouth."

Even a Trojan horse?

Tiara was saying, "I don't suppose we'll be seeing much of each other."

"Just around campus," Sierra countered.

"Naw. I'm dropping out." She sucked in air. "I'm due to get more responsibilities with the company. Makes it hard to continue with classes."

"Oh." Sierra was sorry to hear that, as Tiara was her only friend here. Or anywhere.

Tiara went on, "And both of us know Barnard was always just a means to an end." She added lightly, "But we'll stay in touch."

Sierra knew they wouldn't, though, and at the door, she impulsively gave Tiara a hug, something rare for her. "Take care of yourself."

"You, too, honey. And good luck."

For a long time afterward, her friend's expression – as Sierra looked back at Tiara in the doorway – lingered. Haunted her somehow.

What was it? Anxiety? Sadness? Fear?

Perhaps all three.

But, definitely fear.

8

The following Friday evening, around seven thirty, Sierra met Ethan outside the front gate of Barnard, where they quickly caught a taxi to the Brooks Atkinson Theater.

A block off Broadway between 47th and 8th, the Atkinson shared the side street with the Friedman and Barrymore. A plethora of bars, restaurants, and coffee shops were interspersed, luring theatergoers before and after shows, and during intermissions.

By the time they stepped from the cab, most of the crowd waiting to see *Six* — the hot new musical import from London — had ventured inside the three-story Greek Revival building, save for those politically incorrect daredevils who were grabbing one last smoke.

Inside, the theater decor seemed gaudy to Sierra, even cheap, trying too hard to appear elegant. Yet the Atkinson still commanded a certain respect, its decades of theatrical offerings baked into the high-ceiling moldings, glass chandeliers, embossed gold wallpaper, and red carpet.

Their seats on an end aisle were in the front mezzanine, looking down upon the stage, perfect for viewing a pop concert, which this was, after all: six young women, each representing a wife of Henry VIII, wearing short sexy pseudo-medieval costumes, prancing around on a gold-speckled stage with blue backdrop. Like female Back Street Boys, they sang their stories accompanied by a rock-style back-up band, seizure-inducing flashing lights, and fire-code-taunting pyrotechnics.

At intermission, Sierra and Ethan went next door to a packed bar and grill, the Mean Fiddler, and luckily scored a table another couple had just vacated. Their drinks – hers, an espresso martini; his, Guinness Stout – arrived just as the bar began to thin, folks heading back to their theater seats. They decided not to return to theirs, and instead shared an order of fish and chips.

"Well," Ethan said, "what do you think of it?"

"The martini?" she joked, nursing her second. "Or the fish? Or chips?"

"The *show*."

"What did *you* think?"

"Ladies first."

She nibbled an olive. "I think a better idea would have been a *real* play with songs about the seven wives of Bluebeard."

Deadpan, he said, "Beheadings not grisly enough for you?"

She gestured, nearly knocking her glass over. "You'd have that whole *Les Miserables* thing going...a creepy French seventeenth century château with all those locked doors, skeleton keys rattling on a chain, the seventh wife told by Bluebeard she could go into any room but one. Then curiosity gets the best of her, she unlocks the forbidden door, and finds the dismembered corpses of her six predecessors."

"Is this *your* opinion, or the espresso martini's?"

She ignored that. "Plus, it's a much more satisfying ending, because after the last wife gets chased around the house by her husband with an ax, she manages to kill *him! So* much better than the sixth wife of Henry crowing, 'I survived!' Yeah, right, only because your porky old hubby crippled with gout ran out of energy. Otherwise, *her* head would be in a basket, too."

"You know," Ethan said slowly, gazing into his Guinness as if it were a crystal ball, "I was a bit down, going into this evening, but, by golly, if you haven't managed to lift me out of the doldrums."

She stared at him, noted the tiniest of a smile on his lips, and laughed.

"Well," she said, "*you're* the one who took me to a show about murder."

"Guilty as charged. You ever *see* Les Miz?"

"The movie. We have those in Omaha."

"I'm impressed."

Later, in a cab going back to Barnard, Ethan asked, "Anything planned for this weekend?"

"Why?"

"Just wondering. Thought maybe we could meet up at the library tomorrow."

She shook her head; a text from Mr. Jones had come in during the show. "I have work. Sunday, maybe."

"Work doing what?"

"I...I'd rather not say, if you don't mind."

"I don't mind," he said with a puckish little grin. "Saves me the trouble of acting interested."

She patted him playfully on the arm. "It's only...I just started this job, and don't want to jinx it. On my last one, I got fired the first day."

"I have faith in you. You'll make it to day two, easy."

She liked his dry sense of humor. In fact, she liked him very much.

But in front of Brooks Hall, where they stopped at the door, he made his expectations quite clear.

"Look," he said quietly, "I don't want you to get the wrong idea. I don't need a girlfriend at the moment...kind of licking my wounds after the last one. What I *can* use is a friend...and not a friend with benefits."

Although disappointed, she tried not to show it. "I can live with that. A friend could come in handy about now."

Anyway, she'd always heard the best relationships began slowly by being friends with a guy. And between college and her secretive new job, friendship was what she needed most right now, too.

"Good," Ethan said, clearly relieved by her attitude. "Then text me on Sunday. But not too early!"

"I won't — I mean I will, but not early."

SATURDAY MORNING, per instructions, Sierra took an Uber to Penn Station, where the bag pick-up spot this time was a Peruvian restaurant in the main terminal.

She also came prepared to work on a paper due in psychology class on the subject of psychopathology, i.e., the clinical reasons behind abnormal behavior. This sure wasn't high school.

Hours later, in the suite at the Willard, Mr. Jones – dressed smartly in a three-piece charcoal gray suit – seemed in a good mood...even more so after he'd checked the contents of the white envelope behind the closed door of the bedroom.

When he reappeared, Sierra said, "I was wondering if I might head back later than scheduled, today. Seems a shame I've come all this way and not do some sightseeing."

She paused to gauge his reaction and, sensing no discord, proceeded.

"I'd love to visit the National Gallery of Art," she said, "and the Smithsonian. They're both within walking distance."

"Of course, Ms. Kane," he said pleasantly. "You can change your return ticket at the station. Leave whenever you like. Your return time was only set earlier to make your amount of time on the job as short as possible...for your convenience."

"Thank you."

He raised a cautionary finger. "But the front of the ticket must always remain as is."

"Of course."

His smile was slight but distinct. "I hope you have a fine time at the gallery."

"I'm sure I will." She paused. "Have you ever been there?"

"No."

An awkward silence.

She drew in a breath, let it out. "Is it all right if I leave the hotel now?"

His frown was equally slight. And distinct. "You don't care for lunch?"

"I'd rather catch something around the museum."

He sighed. "Room service *does* get old."

She wouldn't have minded a lifetime of room service, but she said, "I'm glad you understand."

According to her GPS, The National Gallery of Art was a nineteen-minute walk down Pennsylvania with a little jog over to Constitution Avenue. Along the way, at a little coffee shop on a side street, 10th, she ordered a vanilla latte (whole milk and whipped cream), then sat at an outside table to enjoy sunshine unimpeded by tall skyscrapers.

Sierra had not chosen this particular café by happenstance, and certainly not because it got great ratings on Yelp. The establishment's location guaranteed it plenty of patrons – among other buildings nearby, the J. Edgar Hoover Building, headquarters of the FBI, was directly across the street.

Sierra watched a woman in a navy pants suit exit the west side of the massive fortress, descend the wide steps, and jaywalk across, a plastic ID on her lanyard flapping in the breeze.

As the woman approached, Sierra called out, "Excuse me – do you have the time? My cell is dead."

The woman stopped to check her wristwatch, long enough for Sierra to read:

FBI

SPECIAL AGENT

And in fluid, readable cursive: ***Carmen Rodriguez.***

"Three o'clock," the agent replied, about to enter the coffee shop.

"Thank you."

They exchanged nods.

Minutes later, when the woman exited, Styrofoam cup in hand, Sierra asked jokingly, "Something *wrong* with the office coffee?"

The woman smirked. "Makes *this* worth the trip."

And crossed the street again in a wanton display of casual lawbreaking.

Sierra finished her latte, made use of the outside receptacle, and continued on her way.

She might need Carmen Rodriguez some day.

The National Gallery of Art was impressive, from the expansive lobby with its huge central fountain to the nearly incomprehensible collection of art.

One could spend days there, and still not see all the paintings, sculptures, and special exhibits. She confined her first visit to eighteenth— and nineteenth-century French paintings on the main floor, as noted by the museum's app.

As five o'clock neared, she sent for an Uber, and – at the Union Station ticket counter – exchanged her earlier return ticket for one leaving at 6:05 p.m.

While waiting to board, she thought, for a moment, she'd seen Ethan – only a glimpse, before he disappeared among the fast-moving crowd.

But that couldn't have been Ethan, could it? Why would it be? What would Ethan be doing here?

Sierra shook her head, convinced she merely had him on her mind.

9

With Thanksgiving looming, Sierra was at a loss – returning to Omaha for a brief vacation did not seem an enticing option. Ethan was flying back to Kentucky for a few days, and – while he'd said she could accompany him if she liked – he suggested they wait till the longer Christmas break. This would allow plenty of time for her to meet his "mildly dysfunctional family" and for the two of them to escape now and then to do fun things together.

Rather than risk their somewhat shakily defined relationship, Sierra didn't push; but despite her loner ways, she did not relish spending Thanksgiving by herself in a mostly vacated dorm.

So on Thursday she booked a flight to Chicago, where she rented a car at the airport, drove into the city, and checked into the Inter-Continental Hotel on Michigan Avenue in the heart of the Magnificent Mile, Windy City's shopping Mecca.

Though relatively flush due to her courier gig, Sierra did not make shopping her priority. Early Friday morning, she summoned her car, left her cell phone in the room — she'd become increasingly suspicious that her movements were being tracked — and drove out of the city, heading south.

The two-and-a-half hour trip to Peoria, along Highway 55, made her heartsick for the heartland. Despite the autumn chill, she powered down her window to breathe in the fragrance of freshly harvested cornfields.

About halfway to her destination, a pick-up truck fell in behind her — not riding her bumper, but missing plenty of chances to go around her. Most other vehicles had done so, as Sierra carefully maintained the speed limit.

Outside the small town of Chenoa, Sierra veered off the highway onto a vegetable stand's gravel apron. The truck went on by, a man at the wheel, bearded, wearing his cap backward. Nobody special. Relieved, Sierra bought some end-of-the-season ears of sweet corn; she unwrapped one and ate it raw while driving, savoring the flavor.

Soon she was crossing the Illinois River into downtown Peoria. Using a road map picked up at a rest stop – how did people get anywhere before GPS? – Sierra made her way to Knoxville Avenue, not far from the city's center.

On a busy street in a commercial area, on a big unlikely grassy lot across from a car wash, stood the former Home for the Friendless, where Sierra's late benefactor Mary Pearson Stafford had been raised. Though it had been renamed the Children's Home, no orphans now resided within those walls.

The three-story rambling red-brick structure, built in the Georgian-era style, hadn't changed dramatically since it was erected in 1900. Today it was a haven for struggling families, offering a wide variety of social services and youth programs.

Sierra parked in the adjacent lot, walked up the semi-circular driveway to the front of the building and up several wide steps to the elaborately framed, leaded-glass front door. Inside, at a desk behind which a corridor of doors extended and a staircase rose, sat a middle-aged woman with short curly brown hair and large glasses, her white blouse crisp and businesslike, softened by its open neck and a string of pearls.

"How may I help?" she asked with a warm smile; her name tag read CLAIRE. Her voice echoed a little in a structure wearing its age with stubborn pride.

"I understand you have a room displaying historical information about this facility," Sierra said. "Going back to when it was founded?"

"We do indeed," Claire said pleasantly. "It's on the third floor." With an upward nod, she said, "Just follow the directory once you get there."

"Will I need a pass of some kind?"

"You will not. But we do like to have visitors sign in. Just a name will do, unless you would like to receive our newsletter online...in that case, add an e-mail."

Sierra signed just a name, and not her own. She wasn't quite sure why she felt the need for such pretense, but she'd always been good at obeying her instincts.

The woman was saying, "We have an elevator in the back...otherwise..." She nodded toward the open stairs.

"Thank you."

Sierra went up, her right hand gliding along a well-worn railing that had been gripped by so many little hands over the years – including Mary Pearson Stafford's.

On the third floor, after consulting a directory on a stand with a diagram of its many rooms, she walked along the gleaming wood hallway passing a classroom with a dozen attentive teenagers, and then a carefree playroom with toddlers. Most doors were closed on the muffled voices of family counselors, their impressive degrees under their names on bronze nameplates. She hoped they were better at their jobs than her guidance counselor back in Omaha.

The Historical Archives room was rather small, perhaps the sleeping quarters of several children before other rooms were combined into dormitories. Light filtered in through a dormer window, illuminating several long glassed-in cases, lending a certain reverence.

The walls held framed photos of the facility starting with its earliest days, when — according to a placard — the Home for the Friendless began with volunteers taking in eight homeless women and their children, before becoming strictly an orphanage.

Most pictures were taken outdoors with the building looming

behind, children lined up in front, adults — teachers and volunteers — standing sternly to either side. Several nurses held babes in arms.

The glass cases displayed more photos – children in classroom settings, or at play outside, or doing chores in the kitchen. One item caught Sierra's eye – a document whose heading read: *Department of Commerce – Bureau of the Census*. Below, was a subheading: *Fifteenth Census of the United States 1930*. The state filing the paper was identified as Illinois; the county, Peoria; and the name of the institution being tallied, Home for the Friendless.

And, most importantly, listed among the inhabitants of this quaintly termed "abode" was one Mary Pearson Stafford. A notation next to her name stated Mary was a newborn whose mother, Helen Pearson Stafford, "died birthing Mary," and whose father was "Unknown."

The thrill she felt surprised her: here was proof Sierra's benefactor had existed! But the sensation stopped her for a moment. Had she doubted the fact?

Sierra was still staring at the name on the list when an elderly woman entered. With a cane, her white hair twisted in a bun, cloth coat open over a casual sweater and slack ensemble, she seemed strangely youthful for a woman who might well be in her eighties.

Seeing Sierra made the woman smile. "Ah!" the new arrival said, approaching. "Usually when I visit no one else stops by this room."

"You come to the Children's Home often?"

"Oh yes," she said. Her eyes were bright. "I lived here for most of my childhood...before I was adopted."

Despite the cane, and all the years she carried with her, the woman moved easily to the wall of early photos. She pointed a bony finger at a large shot depicting the orphans lined up outside, book-ended by those severe adults.

"That's me," she said. "In 1930...just a little tyke, all of three — Josephine Cutter." She paused. "After the stock market crash, my father stepped off a high ledge, and my mother opened her wrists."

The starkness of that made Sierra's stomach clutch. "I am so sorry."

The old woman shrugged. "Shit happens."

Sierra's mouth popped open, but nothing came out. Finally, a question did: "Did you know Mary Pearson Stafford?"

"I certainly did." Josephine's eyes turned back to the photo and the gnarled finger shifted its position. "Nurse right there is holding Mary in her arms. That infant grew into the closest thing to a sister I ever had. We were inseparable till I was adopted. My last day at the orphanage is with me still. 'Don't forget me, Josie,' Mary said. And..." Her voice cracked. "...I never have."

Sierra, not knowing what to say, gave the woman a moment.

"She's buried here in Peoria," Josephine said, matter of fact, her poise recovered. "In Springdale Cemetery, with the others."

"Others?"

"The other orphans who died in those Depression years – influenza, pneumonia, tuberculosis, and the usual childhood maladies. There's a special place at the cemetery called Lullaby Land where an angel watches over them."

This seemed an unusual final resting place for a wealthy woman like Mary Pearson Stafford to choose. But what other family did Sierra's benefactor have? And these fallen children had been her friends.

Josephine asked, "How old do you think I am? No, don't worry about offending me, not at this late date."

"I would say...the early side of eighty?"

"I'm ninety-six," the woman crowed. She sighed, turning back to the photo. "It heartens me, running into a young woman like you here. Finding younger people these days who care about history is almost impossible – it's as if they think nothing ever happened before they were born. No *wonder* this world keeps repeating its mistakes...."

The old woman was staring at the photo when Sierra bid her goodbye and slipped out.

AT THE CEMETERY, Sierra located Lullaby Land, protected by towering oaks and whispering pines. And Josephine's description turned out to be literal, not metaphorical: an angel indeed watched over the children here, in the form of a large white wing-spread marble statue.

The hundreds of graves fanned out from the angel in a circular fashion, too many for Sierra to hope she'd find Mary's stone in the time allowed for her Peoria visit. Each simple cement ground marker contained a name – older ones were chiseled instead of etched by sandblasting – and date of birth and death.

Often included was the reason the orphan had succumbed – in addition to the maladies Josephine had mentioned were dysentery, smallpox, and measles. And it was heartbreaking to think that now such childhood diseases were preventable through vaccines, or controllable with modern medications.

Sierra had thought the earliest graves would have been closest to the statue, the later ones in outer bands; but their placement seemed random or even arbitrary. Perhaps the graves had originally been given plenty of space, with spots filled in and accommodations tightened up, over the passage of time.

Only by happenstance — unless that angel had influenced her path back to her car — did Sierra spot the elusive grave, whose weather-worn, chiseled marker read:

MARY PEARSON STAFFORD
1930 - 1938
DIED FROM POLIO

10

On the Monday following her weekend visit to Chicago – and Peoria – Sierra stopped by Kim Ly's office between classes. The reception desk remained empty, and she knocked on the closed inner-office door.

At first, Sierra heard what seemed to be a muffled "Goddamnit," followed by a more pleasant, "Come in!"

She entered, closing the door. "Rough day?"

Although seated behind a work-cluttered desk, the woman herself looked impeccable, her black chin-length hair sleek, make-up typically flawless, red suit and white blouse wrinkle-free.

Kim Ly summoned a smile but did not gesture to the visitor's chair. "It's always rough right after a holiday break. We send home well-mannered young women and their parents insist on sending back spoiled brats."

"I'll find a better time..."

Finally, a nod to the chair. "There may not be one — let me silence this." She pushed a button on the desk phone.

Sierra sat.

"You've been a bit of a stranger lately," Kim Ly said, leaning back, tenting her fingers. "How's that restaurant job working out?"

So the administrator hadn't checked up on her contact with the Armenian owner.

"It didn't," Sierra said. "But I have a new job."

"Oh?"

"Yes, as a courier for an NFT company."

Sierra had expected this to generate at least one question, but Kim Ly appeared distracted, eyeing the piles of work before her. "Good...good."

Shifting in her seat, Sierra said, "I flew to Chicago over the weekend. And then I rented a car and drove to Peoria...to visit the former orphanage where Mary Pearson Stafford had lived?"

Now she had Kim Ly's attention. "Go on."

Sierra filled the administrator in quickly but completely, from seeing the benefactor's name listed on a copy of the home's 1930s census to meeting an elderly woman who'd known Mary Pearson Stafford at the orphanage. She concluded with the visit to Lullaby Land.

Kim Ly was frowning. "Not exactly how *I* might have spent my holiday vacation." She paused. "I would even say your actions seem a little on the extreme side – don't you think?"

"Not really," Sierra said. "I did learn something important, after all."

"And what would that be?"

"If Mary Pearson Stafford died at the age of eight – in 1938 – she could hardly have attended Barnard in 1950."

That information hovered over them like a dark cloud waiting for its cue to rain.

Then Kim Ly found a notepad on the messy desk, picked up a pen, scribbled something, tore off the slip of paper and passed it across.

Sierra looked at the unfamiliar name on the note. "Who's this?"

"Our head of health services."

"Do you...think I've gone crazy?"

Kim Ly's chin came up. "I think you may need help."

"Why?"

"Because you seem to have become obsessed with this Mary Pearson Stafford. From the very start, you've fixated for some reason on your scholarship's benefactor."

"That's overstating it."

An eyebrow lifted. "Is it? Didn't you walk *blocks* to locate, and visit, the foundation's address?"

"To thank them for the scholarship."

Kim Ly flipped a hand. "A more normal reaction would be to write a thank-you letter...but then you stole a microfiche from the archives — yes, the custodian informed me."

So there were *two* rats in the basement.

"I was going to return it," Sierra said defensively, adding, "Anyway, the fiche was unreadable. Something really should be done about storing them better."

Rather than address that, Kim Ly pressed on with her evaluation. "And now, you spend your vacation going halfway across the country to a former orphanage...tracking down a grave that for all you know was mismarked, dating as it did to tumultuous early days. You wouldn't say *that* is obsessive?"

Sierra considered the woman's words. "I will admit it's like a...a *blister* I can't leave alone. A loose tooth." A scab.

"*Why?*"

What came out was louder than she intended: "Because something just isn't *right* about that foundation!"

The administrator issued a long-suffering sigh. "Sierra. Please. The head of health services will direct you to someone who can help you."

Sierra realized she wasn't getting anywhere with this woman who had, in a way, also been a benefactor. Why alienate her further?

"Okay," she said. "I will."

"Good."

"But could you get me the names of past Stafford scholarship recipients?"

"Sierra?"

"Yes."

"I think you should leave."

She did.

THAT NIGHT, alone in her dorm room, Sierra couldn't sleep, wondering if the admissions head had been right – that she *was* unnecessarily, even unnaturally, obsessed with Mary Pearson Stafford.

After all, she had once been diagnosed with ADHD, and given Ritalin, though Sierra had always suspected her foster parents at the time would have preferred drugging her to dealing with a rambunctious pre-teen. But maybe something *was* wrong with her.

Sierra was still fretting in the dark, the LED numbers on her bedside clock approaching two a.m., when a faint scratching came at the door.

Sierra was positive she'd locked it! And yet, in the faint glow of moonlight through the windows, she could see the metal doorknob turning, ever so slightly.

She sat up, looking for any makeshift weapon. Since the nightstand lamp would be too unwieldy, she grabbed the large ceramic coffee mug next to it and dropped to the floor in a crouch.

The door opened quietly on a tall, shadowy figure that moved slowly, inexorably, toward her bed. Ready to spring up with the mug and clout the intruder, she heard a whispered, "Sierra? Tiara."

Sierra, relieved but angry, got to her feet. "Jesus, Tiara! What the—"

"Sorry." She was still whispering. "I didn't dare use the phone."

In the ivory moonlight, Tiara looked like an unkempt ghost, hair messy, make-up smeared, her sweatshirt and pants baggy...not at all the glamorous party girl. But this was, after all, the middle of the night, and no party.

Returning the cup to the nightstand, switching on the lamp, Sierra asked, "How'd you get in?"

A weary shrug. "Never returned my key."

"Fine, but you scared the *hell* out of me! What's so important that—"

"Not here," Tiara said, raising a palm. Then she gestured behind her. "Bathroom."

Sierra sighed, got into the confiscated oversize shower shoes, and padded after Tiara down the hall to the communal shower room. Within the echoey chamber, her friend checked each toilet stall and shower for company.

They were alone.

Sierra demanded, "Well?"

Tiara, standing close, had liquor on her breath. "I think maybe somebody wants to kill me."

Sierra laughed, but a nervous one that caught. "Why would anyone want to do that?"

"I'm...I'm not sure. But I swear someone is following me."

The memory of that truck on Highway 55 flashed through Sierra's mind.

"Do you see who?"

"Just that it's always the same car, but too far back to make out the driver."

She narrowed her eyes at her friend. "Maybe you should take it easy on the cocaine."

But her friend's eyes widened, her pupils normal. "I'm *serious*, Sierra! My promotion hasn't come through, and I don't think it ever will."

"What do the people you're working for say?"

Words came out in a rush: "When I call the number I was given, it goes to an answering service. And my messages are never returned."

Anxious to help her upset friend, Sierra did her best, saying, "I could mention this to Mr. Jones, for you, next time I see him..."

Tiara's answer came like a slap: "No!"

"...Okay. Okay."

"I'll...I'll reach out to him myself." She paused. "Didn't mean to snap at you. Or frighten you. I...I just wanted you to *know*, that's all."

"What *else* should I know, Tiara?"

For a moment her friend fell silent. Then: "That girl who was killed in the subway — Emily Stewart? The one whose backpack you have?"

Sierra nodded. Another Stafford scholarship winner. "What about her?"

Tiara nodded. "She was a sophomore when I got here. I took over for her, in her courier role, the way you stepped in for me. And look how she wound up – *dead*."

"That was a mugging gone bad," Sierra said. "Wrong place at the wrong time."

Was she trying to convince Tiara or herself?

"I don't think so," Tiara said.

Suddenly it seemed cold in the bathroom; Sierra shivered. "What exactly are you getting at?"

Tiara drew in air, let it out. "I'm starting to think couriers like us have an expiration date...a shelf life of about a year."

Sierra was still processing that when Tiara added, halfway out the door, "Watch yourself," and was gone.

But her friend's words echoed in the chamber, and Sierra's mind.

She was left with one thing: a certainty that now she *had* to get a list of prior scholarship winners from Kim Ly,to learn if any other Stafford winners had died.

THE FOLLOWING MORNING, Sierra woke up groggy, already late for class. Tiara's middle-of-the-night visit seemed almost like something she'd dreamed – an impossible, crazy dream at that.

She skipped a shower, put on yesterday's clothes, grabbed her backpack, and headed quickly out.

Because the elevator was slow, she took the stairs down as a classmate she recognized from econ was coming up.

"Hey," the classmate asked, "didn't you room with that Tiara for a while?"

The back of Sierra's scalp tingled. "Yes. Why?"

"You haven't heard? She got hit by a car when she was crossing to her apartment last night."

Sierra's intake of breath echoed in the stairwell. "Is she going to be all right?"

"Oh no. I'm sorry. She died." Awkwardly, as they paused separated by a step, this classmate she barely knew touched Sierra's shoulder. "Are you all right?"

Was she?

11

The following Saturday, Sierra used the time on the train to consider what she was going to say to Mr. Jones about Tiara's death. With nearly a week having passed, he would surely have learned of the sad fate of his now former employee.

But should she tell him about Tiara's middle-of-the-night visit? That Tiara had spoken of fearing for her life not long before her death? Or would it be wiser not to mention it? Mr. Jones had to realize Sierra was bound to hear, on campus, what happened to her former roommate.

And if Mr. Jones had something to do with the hit-and-run, he probably already knew about Tiara's visit. Perhaps, for her own protection, Sierra should bring it up herself. Seated on the train, with a thrum of wheels-on-rails accompaniment, she rehearsed various conversations with him in the theater of her mind.

When the Express pulled into Union Station, however, she was still undecided. But one thing she'd learned in her brief stay on the planet: conversations rarely, if ever, played out in real life as they had in her head.

So it was with more than a little trepidation that Sierra arrived at the Willard Hotel suite.

Then, after ushering her inside, Mr. Jones immediately said, "What shocking news about Tiara."

Perhaps he'd spent his morning hours as she had, thinking through what words they might exchange, and had decided to take the offensive.

"Yes," Sierra said, adding, "Tragic."

"Coffee?"

Sugar, cream, with that hit-and-run?

"No, thank you." All the civility of this and the meetings with Mr. Jones that preceded it did not dispel the fear that any drink he offered might be drugged.

He gestured to the couch and they sat.

"I'd been trying to reach Tiara about her new position with the company," her host began. "And when my calls weren't returned, I got in touch with her condo management association, and was told what happened." He shook his head. "Such a promising young life snuffed out by a horrible accident."

That he was still talking about it opened the door for Sierra to lay her cards on the table. "She came to see me the night she died. I may have been the last to see her alive...other than that driver."

"It that right?"

She nodded. "Tiara was upset. She thought you were unhappy with her, and were going to fire her...because she hadn't heard anything about the new position she'd been promised."

Seconds seemed like minutes as Sierra waited for a response.

Finally Mr. Jones sighed. "Tiara wasn't wrong about that. She *was* going to be dismissed."

"Why?"

"Drugs. Alcohol. Partying." He paused. "Apparently she'd become...indiscreet. Sharing with others, outside our circle, what that new position would have entailed."

And just exactly what it "entailed," he clearly was not going to share with Sierra.

"I see," she said, keeping her expression blank.

Mr. Jones continued: "It's simply this – Tiara's trustworthiness had been called into question." He turned over a hand. "This is a competitive business. That's why, rather than using e-mails or texts that could be hacked by rival companies, information is passed by hand on a flash drive."

Which Sierra had long since guessed was what each sealed envelope contained.

"I have to admit," he was saying, "it is disturbing that two of our recent couriers have died. A troubling coincidence....You *do* know about Miss Stewart?"

That he'd brought up Emily before she could was either an indication of candor or cunning.

Sierra nodded. "Tiara told me the about the subway mugging."

Another sigh, brief but appropriately sad. "Miss Stewart was from a small town in Missouri, and was apparently unaccustomed to the realities of life in the...well, big bad city. It was due to that incident that our associates implemented using storage spots at Penn Station, rather than deliver the flash drive to the courier. You see, Miss Stewart had one in her possession at the time she was killed, which was most unfortunate."

Unfortunate for the company, he meant, not Emily.

Sierra asked, "Did you miss out on a purchase because of that?"

He waved that off. "We had time to receive another."

She felt comfortable enough to ask, "Did you ever recover her drive?"

"No."

"Aren't you worried that it's floating around out there somewhere?"

He shook his head. "By the time anyone could break its encryption, the information would be dated. Worthless."

She said, "The NFT transaction would've already taken place."

"That's right." He went on, "After Miss Stewart met such an unfortunate end, I had high hopes for Tiara. Coming from Chicago, she'd be far more street savvy."

A funny way to put it, considering she'd been run down.

His shrug was barely perceptible. "But I suppose, considering her background, Tiara had certain...vulnerabilities."

Sierra, reflexively defending her friend, blurted, "You don't have to be a girl from the projects to take drugs or have bad boyfriends."

She was immediately sorry she'd said it, but Mr. Jones only smiled, gently. "Maybe so. But I'm confident you'll do better than your unlucky friend."

"I'll...I'll certainly do my best."

The smile turned vaguely threatening. "I know you will."

AFTER MR. JONES LEFT, Sierra stayed only long enough to use the hotel note pad and pen, before departing. She had an agenda in mind.

The lobby was bustling with guests on their way to or from some tourist excursion, and lapel-flagged politicians headed to a luncheon meeting or (those flying solo) a possible apolitical rendezvous.

Someone bumped into her. "Oh, I am sorry!"

It was the attractive older redhead, smothered in Chanel No.5, from the elevator on Mr. Jones's floor.

"Hello," Sierra said.

"We have to stop meeting like this," she said with a smile, and headed in the direction of the circular bar.

Sierra frowned to herself, thinking she wasn't pleased to be seen as a regular at the hotel. Outside, dark clouds were moving in, possibly with snow on their minds – it was cold enough for that. Sierra buttoned her coat collar.

She walked down Pennsylvania Avenue, again taking a turn onto 10th. At the coffee shop across from the side of the FBI building, Sierra went in, ordered a small latte, then sat sipping it at a table near the front window.

Midway through her second cup, Sierra began to think Carmen Rodriguez wasn't working this Saturday – or had opted for unsavory government coffee – when across the way the agent descended the steps in the same suit as before (or one like it), coatless, braving the weather.

Sierra's heartbeat quickened. Was she about to make a smart, necessary move...or the mistake of her life? One that might even end it?

When Rodriguez entered, and noticed her, Sierra detected a spark of recognition as the woman moved by. Sierra rose, walked to the counter where the agent had just ordered, stood alongside her, and pressed the note into the woman's dangling hand – the note she had written in the hotel room.

Casually, Sierra exited the coffee shop and continued on to the National Gallery of Art, where she passed through security and proceeded to a room labeled gallery 53, just steps away from the main floor's fountain.

She sat on a bench in front of a large oil painting, "House of Cards," by eighteenth-century French artist Jean Siméon Chardin. It depicted a boy stacking playing cards.

Sierra waited twenty minutes that seemed longer, but remained confident the agent would show. Which Rodriguez did, settling in next to her. Not too close, but close enough for a private conversation. They were, for the moment at least, alone.

"All right," the agent said, with some irritation. "What's this about?"

Both stayed focused on the painting.

"I think," Sierra said, "I may be involved in something illegal."

Sierra proceeded to tell her, as concisely as she could, about her unusual courier job.

When Sierra had finished, Rodriguez stated, matter of fact, "Cutout."

"Yes, I'd *like* to cut out," Sierra said. "But I don't know how."

"No." Her gaze returned briefly to Sierra. "*You* are a cutout."

"What do you mean?"

"A cutout is one link in a chain of communication, and – even if something illegal *is* going on – it's not worth the FBI's time investigating."

Stunned, Sierra asked, "What? Why?"

A tiny sigh from the agent. "Because you are unlikely to lead us to the source, which is almost certainly insulated by other cutouts."

Rodriguez began to rise, but Sierra took hold of the woman's arm, drawing her back down. "Two couriers before me have *died!* And I could be next."

The agent removed Sierra's hand, as if it were a small, annoying bug. "Then you were right to take precautions meeting me. And the longer we talk, the more danger you may be putting yourself in." She paused. "Let me give you some advice."

"Please!"

"The money you're receiving? Pay your taxes on it. Quarterly is best, in this situation." She stood. "Good luck."

"Oh, thanks a lot," Sierra said. "Thanks ever so much."

As the agent walked away, low heels clicking, Sierra – unable to contain herself – called out, "I thought you were supposed to *help* people!"

The words echoed in the chamber but the agent was already around the corner, and the boy in the painting was still stacking cards.

12

Sunday morning, just before noon, Sierra walked briskly along the brick pathway toward Milbank Hall, following her visible breath through the cold air.

The campus was all but a ghost town — students catching zees or attending church (or both), many off on decidedly unspiritual searches for food and fun, others settling for Hewitt Food Hall with an afternoon of study ahead. Even the traffic on Broadway seemed subdued.

Though the administrative offices were closed, the front door of Milbank was open, the building pretty much unpopulated. A janitor – possibly the one she'd encountered in the basement – would be mopping floors and cleaning bathrooms, among other mundane if necessary tasks. That was about it.

Inside, seeing no one around, Sierra stood there quietly on the first floor and listened, taking stock. After a moment came the muffled but distinct clanking of a cleaning cart getting pushed along the hallway on the floor above.

Stealing glances as she went, Sierra made her way to Kim Ly's office door, where – after producing two large straightened paperclips from a jeans pocket – she proceeded to pick the lock.

She was not new to this kind of thing. In her high school days, after taking a YouTube tutorial, she had entered the main office and changed a failing grade in Algebra on the registrar's computer. On another occasion, she'd pilfered some petty cash from the Pizza Palace manager's office — not enough to be missed. But she'd had school clothes to buy.

Normally, Sierra was as law-abiding as the next young woman; but a foster kid learns to do what it takes to survive.

She stepped inside and locked the door behind her.

Even on this overcast day, enough light sneaked in through the windows for her to navigate the receptionist's area. Having worked at the desk months ago while the woman was out sick, Sierra was familiar with the computer, knowing its incredibly unsecure password – the school's motto, sans spaces: followthewayofreason.

That seemed fitting, because what could be more reasonable than Sierra seeking information that might help save her ass?

And this computer would do just as well as Kim Ly's. Both women's stations utilized the same system, which was a good thing, as the administrator might be more likely to realize her computer had been tampered with.

Sierra located the file of Stafford scholarship recipients and – rather than downloading or e-mailing it to herself, which might easily be traced — she printed a hard copy. She went back three decades, gathering twenty-seven names – not bothering with Emily, Tiara, and herself.

Using the interdepartmental file-sharing system, she accessed data from Barnard's Alumnae Center in the Vagelos Computational Science Building. The staff there were aggressive about keeping track of former students – not only graduates, but anyone who'd ever attended Barnard even for a single semester. Donations played a key role in battling the constantly rising cost of running a twenty-first century college.

She opened a spreadsheet of active alumnae, including first name, middle, current surname, and (*yes!*) original surname, along with cell phone numbers, e-mail and/or, mailing addresses, plus the years the women attended Barnard. Sierra began cross-checking her hard copy against the alumnae list. Before long she'd found nineteen of the twenty-seven scholarship recipients among the active alumnae. This made her smile, something she didn't do all that often.

For the remaining eight women, Sierra turned to social media platforms, locating three others who had kept — or returned to — their original surname and, in their personal profiles, listed Barnard as the college they attended.

Turning to sites used by employers who check applicants for police records, lawsuits, or financial problems, Sierra crossed off two more women. The final three garnered multiple hits with identical names, but the sites required a fee for more information, which she dare not do at this computer.

Three Stafford scholarship recipients unaccounted for were hardly enough for Sierra to take to the police or FBI, and even so, to do what? Suggest couriers were being killed, perhaps when they became unreliable or just when their duties were complete?

So either this consortium's use of these women as cutouts was new – perhaps coinciding with the NFT phenomenon — or it really *was* a coincidence that both Emily and Tiara had died in a different, all-too-big-city way. That was when a clanking cleaning cart announced itself.

It rolled closer, closer...then the clatter stopped just outside the door.

Keys jangled.

With no time to shut down the computer, Sierra turned off the monitor and ducked down into the well of the desk, rolling the chair in as close as she could, hoping the janitor wouldn't notice the PC's little green ON light.

If she were discovered, Sierra would not only lose her scholarship, she might be charged with breaking and entering! A high school girl caught changing a grade or stealing petty cash might get a slap on the wrist. A college girl caught in an administrator's office accessing confidential information might get her wrists cuffed behind her and be hauled off to a barred cell.

Footsteps shuffled toward the desk, then moved heavily around the side, keys jingling on a belt, like a prison guard with many inmates to tend. Sierra held her breath.

But the janitor was after the wastebasket, a plastic bag crinkling as he removed it to line the basket with another.

He repeated the process in Kim Ly's office, before finally trudging out, the door closing, re-locking, then the cart rattling away.

Sierra crawled out from beneath the desk. Her breath was coming fast, her heart beating in her ears. She would get out of there while she could.

She turned off the computer, then used tissues from a box on the desk to wipe down the keyboard and mouse – anywhere else she might have touched. She had no reason to think her intrusion would be noted, but why take any more chances?

With the hard copy of Stafford recipients folded and tucked away in a pocket, Sierra listened at the door. Hearing nothing, she cracked it, peered into the hallway – *nothing* – peeked around – *nothing*. She wiped both knobs before slipping out, shutting and locking it behind her.

Though cameras outside caught her coming and going from the building, she felt confident her movements would go unnoticed. After all, someone in security would need a reason to check the recording. And, inside, no security cams took in the door to Kim Ly's office.

After the lack of interest from Agent Rodriguez, she could only think of one person she might confide in about all this, and even seek advice – Ethan. Maybe it was time to tell him everything.

Upon returning to her dorm room, Sierra checked for messages on her cell, having left it behind. She'd texted Ethan last night, asking if he'd be going to the stack that afternoon, but no reply yet. Sierra didn't send another – she didn't want to hound him.

Settling on the bed with her backpack, she was removing her books from the bag, figuring she might as well catch up with her classwork, when she noticed the sewn-on Meowth patch was coming loose. She'd long since lost interest in Pokemon and – rather than resew the patch – she just tore it the rest of the way off. Something dropped onto the bed.

A small thin flash drive.

Could this be the one Emily was supposed to deliver? Mr. Jones said the encrypted drive had been replaced, the data now irrelevant – he didn't need it.

But might *Sierra*? Could the drive be of some use, possibly to get Rodriguez or maybe the police to take a mere cutout seriously?

If so, where to hide the thing?

Again Sierra smiled: *where Emily had, of course.* She got a little travel-size sewing kit from a drawer and went to work.

By Monday, after her last morning class, when Sierra still hadn't heard from Ethan, she got worried something might be wrong. He didn't seem the type to ghost her.

She went over to Columbia and directly to the Registrar's Office in the Student Service Center. After a wait in a queue, she faced a surly middle-aged woman at a windowed counter.

Quickly Sierra summoned a few tears. "I need to find my brother…he hasn't answered *any* of my texts, and our mother is in the hospital."

The clerk, inured to student problems, seemed unmoved. "We can't give out class information."

Sierra kept the waterworks flowing. "But our mother…she may *die* at any *moment!*"

A crack appeared in the woman's wall. "Are you a Columbia student?"

"Barnard."

Four fingers held tight motioned impatiently. "Let me see your ID."

Sierra passed the card to the woman, who studied it, then asked, "What's your brother's name?"

"Ethan Mitchell."

"Your last name is Kane."

"Different fathers."

The woman grunted, and pushed back the card. "Just a moment."

She swiveled to a computer. Keys clicked. A pause, then: "There's no student with that name registered here."

"You're *sure*?"

"I'm sure."

"But I've *seen* his Columbia ID."

The woman's fingers marched again on the keyboard. Another pause, and: "None has been issued in that name."

Stunned, Sierra turned away, another student quickly taking her place and facing an even more irritated welcome.

Outside, Sierra almost staggered to a bench, where she sat in the chill. *What did she really know about Ethan?* If that was even his real name. *Very little.* In giving him the privacy she herself craved, she had apparently allowed herself to be conned.

But why?

Her anger turned to fear. Did "Ethan" work for the NFT consortium? Was it his job to keep an eye on her? To get close and be ready to dispose of errant cutouts?

And she had been about to spill *everything!*

Her cell pinged with a text. From him.

SRY AWOL. When WD U like 2 meet?

13

At Butler, with the week's classes under way, students studying in the second-floor stack took up only a third or so of the space at the tables. Sierra easily staked out two facing seats, which would put the tabletop between her and Ethan. And several seats would be, for now at least, between them and a cluster of students hunkered over books and laptops at the other end.

When Ethan came striding down the center aisle, boyish smile plastered on his face, she could hardly believe his gall – he was wearing a Columbia sweatshirt! Bitter indignation rose like bile within her, but she kept her demeanor cool, her expression pleasant.

As he sat down, she caught a whiff of his aftershave. It stirred memories of conversations that were more pleasant than this one would undoubtedly be.

"So sorry not to get back to you," he began. "I've been super busy."

"No worries."

They were whispering.

"Family crisis," he said with an apologetic shrug. "Couldn't be helped."

Now that she knew he was a liar, everything coming out of his mouth rang false. Why hadn't she seen that?

Sierra smiled sympathetically. "I hope it wasn't anything too serious."

"No, no, everything's fine." He smiled back at her. "What have you been up to?"

"Oh, I've had a very interesting morning."

"Tell me."

"It's a little embarrassing. Are you sure you want me to get into it?"

He frowned in interested support. "Of course."

Sierra leaned forward, elbows on the table, hands clasped under her chin. "Well, all right then. When I didn't hear from you, I went over to the registrar's office – to get your class schedule? And, funny enough, they had no record of you. In fact, no student ID was ever issued in your name."

Ethan, so relaxed before, stiffened. The sparkling eyes hardened, the playful smiled vanished. He suddenly looked older. And perhaps...dangerous?

He lowered his voice. "Sierra, I can explain." He glanced at the students grouped at the end of the table. "But not here. Somewhere we can talk."

She raised an eyebrow. "Somewhere there aren't other people around, you mean?"

"Yes."

She laughed once. "You'd love that, wouldn't you? I could join that exclusive club Tiara and Emily belong to – or *is* it exclusive? Just how big an idiot do you think I am? No, don't answer that."

He gestured gently. "I didn't have anything to do with that."

Mock innocent, she asked, "With what?"

"Their deaths. Not a thing."

Tired of this toying, Sierra asked, flatly, "Who do you work for?"

For a moment he didn't answer. Then he sighed. They were already whispering, but this came even softer: "The Central Intelligence Agency."

She smirked. "Is that the best you can do?"

Ethan produced a wallet and removed a plastic ID. He pushed it across the table to her like the winning card in a game of chance.

Sierra looked down at a photo of the phony seated across from her, a head shot on a blue background with a number running across the top, the government agency's seal at the bottom.

But there was no name, no signature. The reverse side had only a request that, should it be found, the card be mailed to a post office box in DC.

"Our credentials," he said, "are understandably on the restricted side."

She pushed the thing back at him. "Do you know how cheesy that looks?"

He returned the card to his wallet, which he tucked away. "It's real."

She cocked her head. "As real as your student ID?"

His head went to one side as if he'd been slapped; and hadn't he been? "Okay, I deserved that. You don't trust me now, and I don't blame you."

"You are so understanding."

At the other end, students were glancing occasionally at what they apparently took for a messy break-up – not an unusual event on a college campus, but annoying when you were trying to study.

He leaned across as far as the table would allow. "What about that bar on Broadway? Would you be comfortable going there with me? Public place like that?"

Really she should just stand up and walk away. Still, this stranger who'd been Ethan already'd had plenty of opportunities before today to kill her. And, frankly, she was curious to see just how far Prince Charming was willing to take his CIA fairy tale.

"All right," Sierra said. "But there had better be other customers around."

They left the library, exiting onto 114th Street, then walked in silence, Sierra staying slightly behind him.

The small watering-hole did have a few patrons, two female coeds at the bar, backpacks on the floor by their feet as they chatted over glasses of wine, thanks to real or fake driver's licenses. And several high-tops were taken, patrons nibbling the limited bar food.

Ethan asked, "We okay here?"

"Yeah."

But she selected their table.

The same bartender as before came over and took their order — ginger ale for her, tap beer for him — and went off to fill it.

Ethan had his cell out, punched some numbers, then held it to his ear, but sideways. Sierra could hear a woman's voice answer.

"I'm compromised," he said.

"*Put her on.*"

"She'll need to see you."

"*I'll send a link.*"

The call ended.

They sat in silence – and it did feel like a messy break-up, but this was a messy break-up you might not survive – until their drinks arrived.

Ethan accessed his e-mail and set the phone down. Then, after a few moments, Carmen Rodriguez's face appeared on the screen, her expression unreadable. Sierra assumed the app being used was more secure than Skype or Zoom.

"I'm sorry I had to turn you away, Ms. Kane," the FBI agent said, the cell's speaker turned low. "Otherwise I would have been jeopardizing an inter-agency investigation. But you should listen to the man you're with." She paused, then asked, as if to both of them, "Is that enough?"

Ethan looked at Sierra. "*Is* it?"

"Yes...for now."

The screen went black, and he returned the cell to a pocket.

Sierra asked, "Was that *you* I saw at Union Station?"

"Yes."

"And the girlfriend you argued with at the stack?"

"Another agent," he said. "I needed to establish credibility...and gain your sympathy."

"So you stepped on my shoe on purpose."

"And also lifted the pin off your bag," he admitted, "so I could 'find it' and come looking for you. And when I saw that microfiche label, I knew you were looking into the Stafford Foundation."

Sierra sat forward and words flew out. "Are they behind this? Is the foundation involved? Are *they* the NFT consortium?"

He drew in a breath. "That's something I can't share with you at this time."

She studied him. "Okay. How about your real name? Can you share *that*?"

He shook his head. "Sorry."

Sierra shifted on the hard stool. "What *can* you tell me? Maybe start with why you people are interested in the NFT firm that hired me?"

He studied her, then said, "I can give you the broad strokes."

"Please."

He chose his words carefully. "They're using various marketplaces to funnel crypto-currency out of the country to back certain destructive activities."

"What do you mean by 'destructive activities?'"

His gaze was unblinking and anything but sparkling. "Cyberwarfare. Terrorism. Toppling democratic governments."

That stopped her for a while. He waited while she processed what he'd told her.

Finally she said, "What kind of crypto are we talking about? In American dollars, I mean."

"Between fifty and a hundred million for each NFT purchase of basically worthless art."

She goggled at him. "*That* much?"

"That much. I know it sounds unbelievable, but—"

She raised a palm. "No, I read about some guy who paid sixty-nine million bucks for a collage of JPEG drawings. It's crazy, but no...not unbelievable."

He merely nodded.

"Only," she asked, "why use college girls to pass along information on a flash drive? Why not go through some site on the dark web?"

"Who do you think *runs* those sites?"

"Uh...other crooks?"

"Other crooks. Sometimes the old-fashioned, person-to-person way works the best."

Sierra took a sip of her ginger ale. "All right. I believe you. I don't love the way you went about this, but...I believe you."

"Good. And...and I'm sorry."

"Never mind that." She leaned in. "Is there anything I can do to help you expose the people I work for?"

Ethan shook his head. "I'm afraid they're too well-insulated."

Thanks to other cutouts like herself.

Her laugh was a brittle thing. "So, am I destined to end up like Tiara and Emily? Mugged or run down?"

"We're not sure those *weren't* accidents."

Sierra grunted. "*I* am."

They fell silent.

Then something came to her. "What if I could give you one of the encrypted flash drives to crack? You know, see exactly what's on it?"

Another shake of his head. "Three hours is not enough time from when you pick it up in Penn Station till—"

"No, not *my* next delivery...the one Emily was supposed to make to Mr. Jones, but was killed before she could?"

Ethan's eyes showed interest. "You *have* that drive?"

"Right here." She pulled the backpack up from the floor, setting it on the table.

Pointing to Meowth, Sierra said, "I found it under this patch," and proceeded to rip the threads enough to expose the drive.

He reached out a hand tentatively. "May I?"

"Sure." She removed the drive and placed it in his outstretched palm.

As he clutched the small piece of plastic, Ethan's smile was small and tight but those eyes were sparkling again – as if his affection for her might be real. Or for the flash drive at least.

"This," he said, "just might bring the whole consortium down."
"It could do that? How?"
In hushed tones he told her.
"Well," she said, impressed. "You people could *do* that?"
"We can...but you'd be taking an awful chance."
"Aren't I already?"
"Then...you're in?"
"I'm in."

14

On a cold overcast Saturday morning in December, Sierra was picked up in front of Barnard by an Uber driver and taken to Penn Station. There, she retrieved a soft black briefcase at a luggage storage spot and proceeded to the Acela Express platform.

"We'll have eyes on you in transit," Ethan had told her. *"They'll come and go at different stops, so don't look for them."*

She boarded the first-class compartment, giving the occupants only the most cursory glance, and settled into her window seat. As usual, she removed the money from the briefcase, slipped it into her purse along with the other half of her train ticket.

"This must seem like any other trip, Sierra. Do exactly *as you've done on previous instances."*

Toward that end, she had brought along her backpack with class assignments — chapters to read in Psychology, worksheets for Macroeconomics — and, as the train pulled out, she began working on them at her seat's table.

But no matter how hard Sierra tried to concentrate, pages blurred and worksheets made little sense. After an hour, she eased herself up, gathered her briefcase and purse, and ducked into to the lavatory, locking the door.

"I'll show you how to get into the envelope without disturbing the sealed flap."

Using a single-edged razor blade, Sierra slit the fold of a bottom corner of the envelope, just enough to slide out the flash drive.

"If the drive itself looks at all different from Emily's, we'll abort."

But the drives appeared identical.

After making the switch, Sierra used a drop of liquid plastic adhesive to seal the cut and returned the envelope to the briefcase. She flushed the toilet, ran some water, and made her way back.

With this important task completed, she relaxed and returned to her college assignments. Blurring pages came into focus and worksheets suddenly achieved clarity. She was finishing up just as the train pulled into Union Station.

At the Willard Hotel, Sierra walked directly to the elevators. While it would have been easy — even natural — to notice someone loitering, or seated in a chair hiding behind a newspaper, she aimed her eyes straight ahead.

"From the moment Jones answers the door," Ethan had said, *"you must appear normal or he'll sense something is wrong, so for God's sake stay cool."*

She hadn't taken any offense at that, or anyway not much, replying, *"I'm always cool."*

"I know. But it'll help if you convince yourself this is just another run. Same-o, same-o."

Mr. Jones answered her knock and she stepped into the suite.

As usual, her host asked, "How are you this morning?"

"Fine," she replied, per usual.

Sierra crossed the gray carpet to the gray couch and sat, the gray drapes closed behind her, keeping the gray day out.

The urbane figure stood before her while she unzipped the briefcase and withdrew the white envelope, willing her hand not to shake.

He received the offering, strode to the bedroom, and closed the door.

"The hardest time for you will be when he's checking the drive, leaving

you alone to imagine the worst. So keep your mind occupied with something else."

Earlier, passing though Union Station, Sierra had picked up a handful of tourist brochures, which she extracted from her backpack and proceeded to go over.

"If the encryption format and password haven't changed, Jones will be able to open and read our drive, which has the bogus information — NFT marketplace, date, time, number, and scan of artwork to be bought."

"And if he can't open it?" she'd asked.

"Even so, you're almost certainly in no danger in the suite...but you would be when you leave."

"How will I know if your plan works?"

"You won't. Not until the crypto-currency goes into our 'wallet.' You simply go about living your life as usual. But we'll have eyes on you until the purchase goes down tomorrow morning...or doesn't."

"Living my life...unless someone 'simply' manages to kill me."

"Our people are good, Sierra, but you are free to back out."

"And I'd do that why?" Her reply was sarcastic but no joke. "As if backing out would guarantee me a long happy life?"

Ethan hadn't answered quickly, but when his words came, they were dead serious, offering scant solace: "*Maybe your odds would be a little better. A little. And if that's what you decide, no judgment.*"

The door to the bedroom opened and, as Mr. Jones approached, she tried to read his expression, body language, even the pace of his stride. But he seemed his usual, pleasant, businesslike self.

Of course, the man calling himself Mr. Jones might just be a good actor. Or was that a *bad* actor, who was good at it?

"Bored with that art gallery yet?" he asked, eyeing the brochures.

She nodded. "I'm thinking about moving on to the Smithsonian."

Jones shrugged facially. "Well, it's not any more of a walk. And the monuments are at their busiest on a Saturday. It's a good option."

He sat next to her, their legs almost touching. She tried not to tense.

"You know," he said softly, his arm slipping onto the sofa back behind her, "it's not easy trusting others in sensitive work situations like this. And when I find someone I *can* trust, I like to get to know them better."

If he hadn't been able to open the drive, he might be moving in for the literal kill – pretending, for the first time, to flirt when he was really just getting close enough to, what? Stab her, like Emily?

She must not have kept the alarm out of her expression, as he withdrew his arm and he moved away a little.

"Oh, I'm sorry," he said. "I didn't mean to make this uncomfortable for you."

"I'm afraid you have," Sierra said.

Her host's indiscretion was helping explain away any nervousness she might be betraying.

He was saying, "I didn't mean to overstep, and I know that was unprofessional. Do forgive me."

"It's all right."

He tried to make a joke out of it. "I guess you don't find older men attractive."

"It's not that," she replied, and gave him her smallest smile. "It's just...I'm seeing someone I met at college."

His shrug was sheer sophistication. "And I have a wife and a wonderful marriage. But that doesn't mean we can't enjoy each other's company. Thrown together as we are."

Sierra summoned a slightly more encouraging smile. "Let me think about it."

"Of course." He moved the handsome face closer, but not the rest of him. "And even in DC, there are only so many tourist attractions to see."

He stood, straightened himself, and she kept her smile going while he retrieved his laptop, the briefcase, put on his overcoat, and left with a nod and a wink. The latter made her shudder, but he was already gone and never saw it.

Sierra got off the couch, walked into the bathroom, and stared into the mirror, wondering who the stranger was looking back at her.

Omaha seemed a lifetime ago – not four months. The only constant was eventually an older man would put the make on a girl.

Composed again, she gathered her backpack and purse.

In the hallway, a few rooms away, a woman in the blue uniform of the housekeeping staff was at a cleaning cart blocking an open door.

As Sierra headed to the elevator, the woman asked, "And how are you finding everything?"

"Fine," Sierra responded. "Just fine."

"Good to hear," she replied. "Enjoy your stay."

That made Sierra feel better. Now she might actually appreciate the Smithsonian, knowing how well she was being protected. The CIA actually had an agent cleaning that room!

SIERRA SET out for the Museum of Natural History, keeping to her normal schedule, stopping at the usual coffee shop. On this visit, she did not expect to see Carmen Rodriguez, and didn't. But as she ordered her latte to go, she hoped colleagues of the agent were watching.

The museum was practically next door to the National Gallery of Art, separated by a sculpture garden and ice-skating rink. She went in, passing through security, and lingered on the first floor, wandering by exhibits of fossils, stuffed animals, and the evolution of humans. Gazing at a recreation of Neanderthals, she felt envious of how uncomplicated their lives must have been, the occasional sabertooth tiger aside. Then she had a sudden urge to get away from all things dead.

She exited the building and – not trusting who the Uber driver picking her up might prove to be – went off-script by grabbing a cab at the curb whose ride was disembarking.

At Union Station, calmed down somewhat, she exchanged her return ticket for one leaving in an hour. Sierra could have gone sooner, but figured the extra time would allow Ethan's agents to regroup after her quick, impulsive departure from the Smithsonian.

Having a first-class ticket gave her access to the station's Amtrak Club Acela Lounge, which she'd never had the opportunity to use before. Behind its closed doors awaited a haven for the well-heeled – plush leather furniture, wall TVs, luxurious bathrooms, among other amenities. After helping herself to a snack and soda, she settled into a chair.

Only two other people shared the waiting area: a Japanese businessman lost in his laptop, and a middle-aged woman yakking about her kids on her cell. Sierra watched and waited, resisting the urge to sleep. Putting herself in a helpless state would not, she knew, be a wise move.

But later, on the train, exhaustion had its way with her, and she fell into a deep sleep, from which she woke only when someone shook her.

Startled, she sat upright.

"I'm sorry," the female attendant said. "We pulled into Penn five minutes ago and you weren't responding to my voice."

Groggy, Sierra managed, "Thank you."

Outside, she welcomed the frigid night weather, big beautiful white flakes coming down as if heaven sent. She again avoided an Uber and caught a cab. The ride was pleasant, the city resembling a sparkling Christmas card, snow creating halos around blazing lampposts. No exhibit at the Smithsonian matched it.

At last, sequestered in her doom room, with her desk chair propped against the locked doorknob, Sierra texted Ethan: *I'm back (happy emoji). C U tomorrow?*

Almost immediately came: *Noon. Milbank Hall.*

Noon – the time the NFT buy would go down.

Sierra stripped to her underthings, then settled beneath the bedcovers. Her role had been played out with no apparent repercussions. She just had a little longer to wait.

Her mind turned to Ethan's text. Why weren't they meeting at the stack as they always had? Why Milbank Hall? Granted there wouldn't be many students around on Sunday, especially with the winter weather. And there *were* secluded benches among the trees and foliage for her and Ethan to talk privately.

She sat up.

But what if the text hadn't really come from Ethan? What if his cell ID had been spoofed?

What would she be walking into?

15

Mid-morning Sunday, after a fitful night, Sierra arose, dressed, then made a brief visit to her floor's community shower room, brushing her teeth and scrubbing her face. She would've liked to have taken a shower, but was discouraged by the memory of horror movies where bad things happened to young women behind plastic curtains.

Back in her room, seated on the bed, she stared out the window onto 116th Street. The snow, so glorious last night, had long since stopped and evolved into a slushy, dirty mess – Mother Nature's paintbrush no match for big-city wear and tear. A few pedestrians trudged along the indifferently shoveled sidewalks, out to grab a coffee and bagel, or the morning papers, their lives proceeding in an enviably mundane fashion.

With the noon deadline approaching, Sierra put on her winter coat and left her room, went outside, and stood in the cold behind a corner of Barnard Hall where she could view the main gate of the college.

Ethan arrived a little ahead of time, passing under the wrought-iron arch, turning right toward Milbank Hall where they were to meet in the front courtyard. She waited till he'd disappeared around the brick pathway's bend, then left through the gate, where she hailed a taxi going south on Broadway.

At nearly one o'clock, she was dropped in front of Kim Ly's apartment house across from Gramercy Park. By now the NFT buy would, or would not, have gone down.

She rang the bell on the intercom. It took three tries before Kim Ly's voice came through.

"Who *is* it?" the woman demanded, sounding agitated.

"Sierra Kane."

"It's a bad time," Kim snapped. "I'm in the middle of something."

An NFT purchase that had not gone well, perhaps?

"Oh, okay," Sierra said lightly. "It's just that I thought you might be missing something."

"...Such as?"

"Maybe seventy-five million dollars in crypto-currency?"

The door unlocked with a *click!*

Sierra went in, finding Kim Ly's door waiting ajar. Inside, the admissions head waited in the white front room. The familiar surroundings that now seemed to Sierra a memory of some distant past. Her benefactor stood – arms folded, chin high, eyes narrowed – in a black dragon-decorated kimono under which white silk pajamas were barely glimpsed, red satin slippers peeking out like daubs of blood.

As Sierra approached, the head of admissions said guardedly, "I'm listening."

"Could we sit down?"

The woman paused, nodded, gestured to the kitchen table.

When they had settled across from each other, Kim Ly held out a graceful hand. "Cell phone."

Sierra complied. But the phone she passed across was her old dead one. The new perk, duct-taped to her upper arm beneath a loose black sweater, was recording.

Kim removed the dead phone's memory card. And, when she stared at Sierra's chest, the younger woman lifted her sweater to show she wasn't wearing a wire.

"Well?" Kim said. "Where's the money?"

"I have it," Sierra said.

"I assumed as much."

"Mr. Jones should have changed his encryption process after Emily's flash drive went missing. Because I found it."

"Did you."

Sierra continued: "Barnard has a decent computer science department...but Columbia? Wow. And it's amazing what some of those tech guys will do for a smile and a promise."

Kim Ly's response was to arch an eyebrow.

Sierra said, "I had Emily's drive doctored with new information, which I gave to our mutual friend, Mr. Jones, instead of the one I was supposed to deliver. And when the buy went down? All that money went into *my* crypto wallet."

Kim Ly just stared for several moments, then asked, "How much do you want?"

"I'm not greedy. A million would be fine. I don't particularly want to be hunted for the rest of my life. Call it a finder's fee."

Kim Ly's upper lip curled into a sneer. "What makes you think you can blackmail me?"

Sierra shrugged. "If you're the top of this food chain, it's a minimal expense. If you're just another rung up the ladder, I would say some very bad people are likely to be coming after you...of course you know about that better than I."

The sneer disappeared. Was that fear in this confident woman's eyes?

"All right," Kim Ly said. "How would you propose I pass this 'finder's fee' along to you?"

"Sometime this coming week, when you've been able to arrange a buy, call me to your office during school hours. Then you can tell me when, where, and what to purchase, using all but one million of the seventy-five in my wallet. This time *you* can be the courier."

Kim Ly's smile was one of mild amusement, but her gaze was fixed on Sierra like a sniper lining up a target. "I seem to have underestimated you, Ms. Kane. I'd assumed you'd be as pliable and gullible as Emily and Tiara."

"And as easy to dispose of?"

Kim Ly frowned. "Excuse me?"

"Well, not you personally, of course. You directed someone else to remove your previous two cutouts. Mr. Jones, maybe? But probably some specialist in this kind of thing."

Kim Ly sat forward, eyes and nostrils flaring. "I had *nothing* to do with the deaths of those young women!"

A *whump* followed by a *crack* startled them both, as the front door burst open.

Carmen Rodriguez – yelling "FBI!" – rushed in first, followed by two men, bold yellow Bureau insignia on the insulated navy jackets of all three. They held guns in two hands, barrels up but no less threatening.

"Kim Liem Ly," Rodriguez said, approaching the seated women, "you are under arrest. You have the right to remain silent..."

As the agent continued with the *Miranda* warning, the head of admissions glared at Sierra, then through clenched, feral teeth came a soft, clipped, "Stupid little fool."

Rodriguez asked Kim Ly, "Do you understand the rights I have just read to you?"

Kim Ly nodded.

"Out loud, please," Rodriguez said.

Sierra – reduced to a silent spectator – thought, *At least the agent said "please."*

"I understand," Kim Ly said. She was still seated. "Do *you* understand I want my attorney?"

"You'll have an opportunity to arrange that," Rodriguez said, "where we're going."

And hauled the woman up and cuffed her hands behind her.

Sierra rose and moved away from the table, stunned by the swiftness and ferocity of the uninvited guests. The two male agents were already searching the apartment, seizing papers and electronics while Rodriguez escorted Kim outside.

Sierra retreated to the white leather couch.

Shortly, Ethan arrived in suit and topcoat, looking nothing at all like a college student.

He joined Sierra on the couch. Something wounded was in his voice as he asked, "Why didn't you meet me? You worried the hell out of me."

"I—I thought your text might have b—been spoofed," she stammered, thrown by his transformation, and a little intimidated. She couldn't bring herself to say she hadn't been sure she trusted him and had decided to visit – and ensnare – Kim Ly on her own.

He didn't pursue it. Instead he said, "We suspected Ms. Ly was either close to the top of the consortium or behind it herself. That investigation will go on. We do know she was using her position to hire student cutouts. If you'd kept our noon date, I was going to ask you if you'd wear a wire and see her. What happened here?"

She filled him in quickly.

Ethan shook his head. "Damn. Too bad that conversation wasn't recorded. You can testify about it, of course, but having the real thing would make our job a lot easier."

"Oh, I got that on my cell," Sierra said casually. "It's taped to my arm – I recorded it all." She gave him a sweet innocent smile. "Will that help?"

He grinned. "So I'm just another dope who underestimated you, huh, Sierra?"

"Oh, it's not an exclusive club."

BY MID-AFTERNOON, both Kim Ly and (Ethan informed her) Mr. Jones were in custody, and Sierra was back on campus, in her room, flush with a sense of relief and a feeling of pride in the role she'd played, exposing the consortium. She felt at ease with herself in a way she hadn't since first getting involved as a cutout.

She undressed, got into her bathrobe, gathered her plastic shower caddy, and padded down the hall toward the communal shower room for a much-needed cleansing, both physical and emotional. En route, a scent tickled her nostrils.

A whiff of perfume in the hallway was hardly unusual in the dorm, or it wouldn't have been on a Friday evening when students were heading for a night on the town. But on a Sunday afternoon?

And in any case the aroma would be more typical of young women – perfumes like Euphoria, Be Delicious, Romance, or Love Story. Not an expensive one like Chanel No.5.

And it hit her.

Kim Ly hadn't been behind Emily's death or Tiara's! But Sierra thought she knew who the killer was…and who might be stalking her right now….

She went into the shower room slow and careful, knowing the creaky door would announce her. No one was tucked against the inner wall on either side of that door, and the outer shower room area was unpopulated.

She seemed to be alone.

The rectangular configuration of the chamber included, up front, four sinks across from four more sinks; and in back, four stalls opposite four curtained shower cubicles, in silent disuse. Her sense of relief, that ease she felt, was replaced now by an all-too familiar paranoia. Steeling herself, she peeked under each toilet stall, looking for feet. Then she proceeded to draw back every shower cubicle curtain, making sure she really was alone, ready to react if she wasn't. The perfume scent was not present in here, but it clung to her nostrils, spurring her on.

Stepping into the first shower, Sierra did not disrobe, nor set down her caddy, but turned on the hot faucet, the shower head spraying. She left it running as she edged back out, drawing the curtain closed.

Entering the toilet stall directly across the way, she shut herself in and stood on the seat, which gave her a high view of the chamber but, if she hunkered down, kept her invisible between occasional glances over, should her instincts be right that a deadly intruder was stalking her.

A few endless minutes later, the door from the corridor creaked open, then closed.

Risking a peek above the top of her stall before ducking back down as she perched precariously on the seat, Sierra made out a figure in black pants, gray hoodie up, coming slowly down the line of stalls, but bending to check each one.

The intruder moved past Sierra's hiding place before doubling back to stand facing the curtained shower cubicle, from which steam rose as hot water flowed. In the overhead light, a knife blade glinted, poised to strike, held in one taut hand, the other reaching to yank back the curtain.

Sierra stepped down quietly from the seat and edged out of the stall, and the figure — either hearing or sensing her — whirled, and Sierra whacked the would-be assailant in the face with the caddy, its contents — shampoo, conditioner, soap, razor — flying, along with the knife, which jumped from the intruder's hand and spun across the tile floor toward the sinks.

On her way to the floor, the sophisticated Chanel No.5-wearing redheaded woman from the Willard Hotel glared back at Sierra – a lovely face distorted into a hateful, crazed mask.

But the force of the blow had not been as effective as Sierra had hoped: seeing her suspicions confirmed had cost her a split-second of hesitancy that made the difference between knocking the redhead down and not out.

Sierra jumped over the fallen woman to claim the weapon, but a hand grabbed her ankle, jerking Sierra to the cold tile floor, onto her back, and then the woman was on top of her, strong fingers gripping the younger woman's throat.

Choking, Sierra brought her knees up into the woman's midsection, thrusting with both legs, tossing her off, the strangling hands releasing as the redhead fell backward.

Both women scrambled to their feet.

Enraged, the redhead rushed Sierra, pushing her back against the sinks, then moving in with a flurry of fists. Sierra blocked the blows with her elbows and retaliated the same way, a left elbow smashing the woman's nose, blood spurting, a right elbow crushing into her throat, Sierra's would-be killer stumbling back, and now it was the assailant who was choking.

Quickly, Sierra maneuvered behind her, and – using a headlock – wrestled the squirming woman to the floor, and sat on her back. She yanked free her robe's sash and tied the redhead's wrists behind her. Like Rodriguez had cuffed Kim Ly.

Good thing she'd filled her phys ed requirement with that self-defense class.

Two giggling girls burst into the bathroom and froze, agape. They looked unsure about just what exactly they were interrupting.

"Call the police," Sierra commanded. "Then get campus security."

The pair backed out, their slapping flip-flops accelerating down the corridor.

"Now," Sierra said to her captive, "just who the hell *are* you, lady?...And *who* the *fuck* wears Chanel No.5 to a murder?"

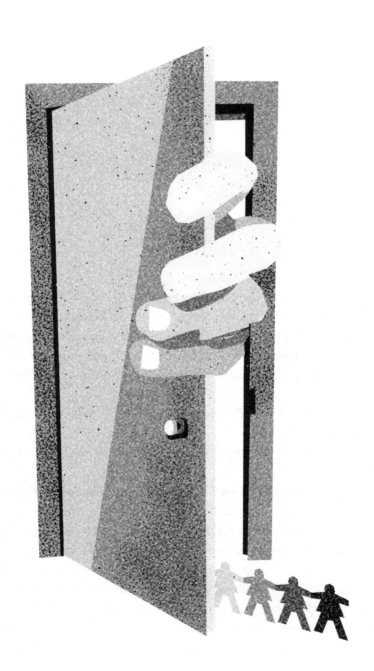

16

A few days after the shower room incident, Sierra and Ethan were seated at one end of a table in a small conference room on the third floor of the corner building at East 42nd Street and Madison Avenue. This was where, nearly four months before, she had gone looking for the offices of the Mary Pearson Stafford Foundation.

"Why meet here?" Sierra asked. She'd half-expected the dark little bar on Broadway.

"It's more convenient," Ethan said, "than traveling to Langley for debriefing."

"I wouldn't mind a tour of the CIA headquarters in Virginia."

"Perhaps one day you'll get one."

"You were about to tell me," she reminded him, "just who tried to kill me in my dorm's bathroom."

"Her name is Vanessa Anderson," Ethan said, matter of fact. "She's the wife of Richard Anderson, who you knew as 'Mr. Jones.' I should add that she's wife number three. According to her statement, she knew nothing about her husband's work for the consortium. She rather tragically misread the situation, taking his meetings with young female couriers as affairs. She assumed the Barnard girls were prostitutes or pick-ups."

Sierra made a sound that wasn't quite a laugh. "I can see how she might think that of him. He came on to me on my last visit. But why didn't she kill *him?*"

"I hope that's a rhetorical question, because I can't answer it. Anderson appears to be fairly high up in this, Kim Ly possibly near or even at the top of the food chain. You may have been closer than we thought, maybe one link away."

Sierra buried a shudder in a shrug. "The cutouts – the couriers – may have been the only buffer."

"I can tell you this much," he said. "It led to the Company...that's the CIA...taking down a major terrorist cell overseas. Which you'll have played an integral part in breaking up. For that we're grateful. *I'm* grateful."

"Better than waiting tables."

That made him smile. "Kim Ly is well-regarded at Barnard. Has there been any blowback there for you?"

"A few whispers, some dirty looks. What happened in the showers was bad enough before the rumor mill got hold of it. The police hauling a middle-aged woman in a hoodie out of a dorm doesn't happen every day."

"True."

"At least the story your people put out about Kim Ly and tax evasion seems to be getting traction. But I'm sure some students and staff think I had something to do with the condo raid, after the media reported me being there when it went down."

"People have short memories. Life will get back to normal."

She had no idea what normal was – going to her classes, yes, but the rest of it had been a ride. A bumpy one.

"I'll finish out the semester," Sierra said, "but my grades have taken a nosedive. I certainly won't get offered another scholarship, not even if I contacted Mary Pearson Stafford by *ouiji* board to explain myself."

"Why go to that extreme?" Ethan said with a tiny grin. "When you can ask her in person?"

"Very funny."

"No joke. She's here. In the next office."

He got up and went out, leaving Sierra to sit in puzzlement for several minutes. When Ethan returned, he opened the door for a striking older woman in a stylish navy suit with a white silk blouse and tasteful touches of gold jewelry, her silver hair beautifully coifed, make-up subtly done.

"Hello, Sierra," the dignified doyenne said, taking the chair next to her.

"*Josephine*?" Sierra asked, dumbfounded – this was the "old lady" she had encountered at the Historical Archives room at the Children's Home! "*You* are Mary Pearson Stafford?"

"Yes, dear. Alive and quite well." She was standing firmly without the help of a cane. "And do call me Mary. Everyone does. That or Ms. Stafford."

Was *no one* who they appeared to be?

Cheeks hot with indignation, Sierra said, "What about all that claptrap you laid on me in Peoria? Was it all lies?"

A gentle shake of the head. "All true and not in the least claptrap."

The refined figure glanced back at Ethan, who pulled out a chair for her to sit beside the flabbergasted Sierra.

The woman said, "I *did* know my Mary at the orphanage, and we *were* like sisters. And, when I was adopted, I felt terribly guilty about leaving the child, even though it was through no fault of my own. Her death a few years later... from polio at the age of eight...only increased that guilt."

Sierra had turned to face the woman. "Then that *was* Mary's grave I found. But now you claim...you're *her*?"

"Let me explain, dear, please," Mary said. "The summer after high school, I worked as a domestic for a wealthy widow in Peoria, who offered me a scholarship at her alma mater – Barnard College – which of course I gratefully accepted. But, disliking my name much as you did yours, I enrolled as Mary Pearson Stafford." She paused.

"One might say, establishing my import/export business in her name, and later the scholarship fund, was my way of keeping Mary alive. That and changing my name legally to hers."

"Then why 'end' her life," Sierra asked, "for a second time? Your foundation says you died years ago."

A tiny smile; a tiny sigh. "By the early 1980s, I was ready to retire. I sold my import/export business, but continued to run the scholarship foundation from Peoria. I still do, working alone but for some minor secretarial help."

"So you knew about me," Sierra said. "It was no coincidence, meeting me at the Children's Home."

"Not a coincidence, no." She nodded to the CIA agent standing dutifully behind her. "Ethan here contacted me saying my girls were being used as couriers for nefarious purposes, and I agreed to help in any way I could."

Ethan said to Sierra, "I felt you might succeed where we'd failed, in identifying and exposing the co-conspirators in the consortium."

Sierra asked him, "So you knew I'd gone to Peoria?"

He nodded, looking vaguely embarrassed. "We had eyes on you as soon as you landed in Chicago."

"And the driver of that red pick-up truck?"

"One of ours. Truck and driver."

"He fooled me," Sierra admitted, then grinned and shook a finger at him. "But you couldn't put that female agent past me! The one playing housekeeper at the Willard."

"What female housekeeper at the Willard?"

"You really didn't...?"

"We really didn't. But if it made you even a little more comfortable, I'm glad."

Mary, glancing between the two young people and seeming to sense something, said, "I'm sure you two have more to talk about, and I have a plane to catch."

Ethan helped the woman out of her chair. "I'll have someone drive you to the airport."

"I'm perfectly capable of getting myself there, young man. You might have someone whistle up a taxi for me."

From a small clutch purse, Mary withdrew a business card, which she handed to Sierra.

"My dear, when things have settled down, we can talk at more length, if you like. You may call me any time, and perhaps even visit me in Peoria."

Getting to her feet, Sierra said, "Thank you. Thank you for everything."

The dignified woman hugged Sierra gently, quickly, but the warmth of the gesture was obvious. Some emotion washed up onto the shore of Sierra's island.

"And please know," Mary said, "that you have a place at Barnard as long as you wish." Then she added cryptically, "Unless, of course, your path leads somewhere else."

"Thank you, Ms. Stafford," Sierra said. "I'll do my best to make you proud."

"I already am, my dear."

After Mary was escorted out, Ethan returned and took the chair next to Sierra, who asked him, "Did she mean anything by 'another path?'"

"Yes. We told her we're willing to back a fellowship for you with the CIA."

Sierra's eyes widened. "Seriously?"

"Yes, I, uh...told her you'd demonstrated the kind of qualities the Company...not the consortium...is looking for. But you'd have to get your grades up, and transfer to an MSI college."

"MS what?"

"MSI – Minority Serving Institution. There are hundreds throughout the country that qualify. And we offer scholarships, too."

"Which college is closest to you? To, uh, Langley I mean?"

"University of DC, across the Potomac."

Sierra gave him a look he understood. "I suppose the CIA has strict rules about employee fraternization."

"It does. Of course, you're not an employee *yet*..."

She leaned toward him. "Well then, don't you think it's about time I knew your real name?"

He hesitated, then sighed. "Maynard Philpott."

"Oh."

"Maynard *Eugene* Philpott. The Third."

She twitched a smile. "Ever consider changing it?"

ABOUT MAX ALLAN COLLINS

MAX ALLAN COLLINS was named a Grand Master by the Mystery Writers of America in 2017. He has earned an unprecedented twenty-three Private Eye Writers of America "Shamus" nominations, many for his Nathan Heller historical thrillers, winning for *True Detective* (1983), *Stolen Away* (1991), and the short story, "So Long, Chief."

His classic graphic novel *Road to Perdition* is the basis of the Academy Award-winning film. Max's other comics credits include "Dick Tracy"; "Batman"; and (with artist Terry Beatty) his own "Ms. Tree" and "Wild Dog."

His body of work covers film criticism, short fiction, songwriting, trading-card sets, and movie/TV tie-in novels, including the *New York Times*-bestseller *Saving Private Ryan*, numerous *USA Today*-bestselling CSI novels (with Matthew V. Clemens), and the Scribe Award-winning *American Gangster*. His non-fiction includes *Scarface and the Untouchable: Al Capone* and *Eliot Ness & the Mad Butcher* (both with A. Brad Schwartz).

An award-winning filmmaker, he wrote and directed the Lifetime movie *Mommy* (1996) and three other features; his produced screenplays include the 1995 HBO World Premiere *The Expert* and *The Last Lullaby* (2008). His 1998 documentary *Mike Hammer's Mickey Spillane* appears on the Criterion Collection release of the acclaimed film *noir*, *Kiss Me Deadly*. The Cinemax TV series *Quarry* is based on his innovative book series.

Max's novels include a dozen–plus works begun by his mentor, the late mystery-writing legend, Mickey Spillane, among them *Kill Me If You Can* with Mike Hammer.

Barbara and Max Collins live in Muscatine, Iowa; their son Nathan works as a translator of Japanese to English, with credits include video games, manga, and novels.

ABOUT BARBARA COLLINS

BARBARA COLLINS made her entrance into the mystery field as a highly respected short story writer with appearances in over a dozen top anthologies, including *Murder Most Delicious, Women on the Edge, Deadly Housewives* and the bestselling *Cat Crimes* series. She was the co-editor of (and a contributor to) the bestselling anthology *Lethal Ladies*, and her stories were selected for inclusion in the first three volumes of *The Year's 25 Finest Crime and Mystery Stories*.

Three acclaimed collections of her work have been published – *Too Many Tomcats* and (with her husband) *Murder — His and Hers* and *Suspense – His and Hers*. The couple's first novel together, the Baby Boomer thriller *Regeneration*, was a paperback bestseller; their second collaborative novel, *Bombshell* – in which Marilyn Monroe saves the world from World War III – was published in hardcover to excellent reviews.

Barbara also has been the production manager and/or line producer of several independent film projects.

ABOUT THE PUBLISHER

NeoText publishes original illustrated short fiction and narrative non-fiction by some of the best authors and artists of today. Devotees of pulp fiction, pop culture and narrative art, we explore innovative ways to embrace creative storytelling in the digital age. For information on our latest releases, please visit us at NeoTextCorp.com

Made in United States
Orlando, FL
30 June 2024

48473625R00075